SPEEDWELL

Books by the same author

Maroo of the Winter Caves

Picture books

Make It, Break It
Rob Goes A-Hunting
The Sand Horse

SPEEDWELL

Ann Turnbull

CANDLEWICK PRESS
CAMBRIDGE, MASSACHUSETTS

First U.S. paperback edition 1994
First published in Great Britain in 1992 by
Walker Books Ltd., London

Library of Congress Cataloging-in-Publication Data

Turnbull, Ann. Speedwell/by Ann Turnbull.

Summary: With her father away looking for work and her
mother weighed down by the troubles of the Depression of
the 1930s, Mary wants to help her family and sees her
father's racing pigeon Speedwell as her best hope of doing so.
ISBN 1-56402-112-2 (hardcover)
[1. Homing pigeons—Fiction.   2. Pigeons—Fiction.
3. Depressions—1929—Fiction.   4. England—Fiction.]
I. Title
PZ7.T8493Sp 1992   [Fic]—dc20   91-58757
ISBN 1-56402-281-1 (paperback)

10 9 8 7 6 5 4 3 2 1

Printed in Great Britain

Candlewick Press
2067 Massachusetts Avenue
Cambridge, Massachusetts 02140

For Linda

I should like to thank everyone who helped me with
my research into pigeon racing, especially
Angela Harris and Wilson Stephens.

Chapter One

"He ... that ... h-h-he—"

"Heareth," said Miss Lidiard. "Start again, please, Arnold."

"He that ... heareth ... you ... h-h—"

"Heareth." Miss Lidiard's fingers drummed on her desk top.

The class sighed and shifted. Mary hid the crossed fingers of her left hand in her lap and turned the page of the Bible with her right. She glanced over her shoulder at Arnold Revell. He sat hunched over the undersized desk, his face furrowed in concentration, mumbling as he traced the words with a finger.

"Speak up, Arnold," said Miss Lidiard.

The class tittered. Olive Jennings, who was sharing the Bible with Mary, leaned forward. Her plait tickled Mary's cheek. "Dopey," she whispered, enjoying the diversion.

But Mary wriggled with impatience. She wasn't in the mood for Miss Lidiard's Arnold-baiting. It was the last lesson of the day. The last few minutes. She'd had her fingers crossed all afternoon. All she wanted now was to hear the bell.

Miss Lidiard tired of tormenting Arnold.

"Doris Brown," she said.

"Hethathearethyouhearethme . . . ," gabbled Doris. *Show-off,* thought Mary.

"And he that despiseth you despiseth me and he that despiseth me despiseth Him that sent me—"

The bell clanged.

"Thank you, Doris," said Miss Lidiard. She closed her Bible.

Benches scraped as the class stood up.

"Hands together, eyes closed," said Miss Lidiard.

Mary obeyed, keeping her fingers still furtively crossed. The familiar words came to her tongue unthinking while her mind prayed, "Please, let me get home in time to see it hatch."

"Goodbye, children."

"Goodbye, Miss Lidiard."

They were free. Out through the doorway and into the playground.

"Want a pear drop?"

Olive passed Mary a paper bag. Inside were a few yellow sweets, stuck together. Mary prized one free, bringing bits of paper with it.

"Thanks."

She sucked the sweet slowly, spinning it out, feeling its cough-medicine smell going up the back of her throat. She didn't get many sweets, not now that Dad was out of work, but Olive's family owned the sweet shop in town.

"There's your sister," said Olive.

Mary removed a fragment of paper bag from her tongue. "I'd better go. See you!" She ran to join Phyl.

"Only three more days!" said Phyl.

Next Thursday, the ninth of May 1930, would be a special day for Phyl. It was her fourteenth birthday and she would be leaving school forever.

Mary was jealous. She breathed pear drop scented breath at her sister.

"Get off!" Phyl giggled, pushing her. "What have you got your fingers crossed for?"

Phyl never missed anything. Mary hid her left hand behind her back.

"I don't."

"You do. I know! The squeaker."

"I want to see it hatch. I always miss them."

"You and your pigeons," said Phyl.

They walked home fast. Both were hungry; they had had only a hunk of bread for their lunch, and that was hours ago.

They ran down Lion Street and turned at the arched passageway between their house and the Lloyds'.

The fragrance of soup drifted from the kitchen.

Mary was tempted to stay with Phyl and follow the smell to its source. But the possibility of seeing the squeaker hatch was too exciting. She ran down the garden path, between the line of damp laundry and rows of leeks, to the loft.

Dad had built the loft. It was a good one, strong and roomy and clean smelling. It faced away from the house, so she couldn't see the pigeons until she turned the corner. But she heard their cooing. The front of the loft was slatted to let air in, and behind it she saw the birds moving around.

It felt strange not to find Dad here, checking the food and water, talking to the birds, making notes in the book that hung on a nail inside the door. But Dad had gone to Midhope today, looking for work, and wouldn't be back till late. Today it would be Mary's job to let the hens out for their exercise while the cocks were sitting.

She opened the door and went in. The birds knew her, and she caused only a slight shifting and ruffling of feathers. She moved softly, as her father had taught her. At the end of the row was Lenin, sitting on his nest bowl. And she was too late! The eggshell lay broken on the floor, and underneath Lenin's breast feathers she caught a glimpse of down.

"Come on, let's see you," she said. She lifted Lenin, who fluffed up his feathers and looked outraged, and there it was, a tiny thing with sealed eyes and an oversized lump of a beak. Its down was not quite dry.

"Only missed you by half an hour, I reckon," said Mary.

There was a tapping at the loft door: Lennie, her little brother.

"I want to see the squeaker."

Mary let him in, shushing him, slowing him down.

"Can I hold it?" Lennie's hands reached out longingly.

"Not now. When it's older."

"Can I hold the Lennie one?" Lennie was convinced that Lenin was named after him and he had a special fondness for the bird.

"No. He's getting angry." Mary put the struggling bird down by the nest bowl. Lenin climbed back in and spread himself protectively over the newly hatched bird and the second egg, which would hatch in a day or two.

"You can hold the Gaffer," said Mary.

The Gaffer was the oldest bird in the loft, and the tamest. He didn't race anymore because he had once fractured a wing and it had healed crooked, but he had been a great racer in his time and Dad kept him for breeding.

He was sitting on a ledge now, close to Mary, watching. Mary picked him up, feeling the weight of him, almost as much as the one-pound bags of sugar Mum sent her to fetch from Greening's. She passed him to Lennie.

The Gaffer sensed Lennie's awkwardness and struggled. Mary showed her brother how to hold him, with one hand curved around his breast, the other around his rear, and the legs held between two fingers.

"Your hands are a bit small," she said.

"I like him," said Lennie. But the Gaffer fluttered, and he let him go.

Mary heard Phyl shouting outside: "Mum says do you want any supper or not?"

Mary opened the door a crack. "I just have to let these hens out."

"Hurry up, then. She's in a bad mood."

"That egg's hatched," said Mary.

Phyl pulled a face. She didn't like pigeons, especially newly hatched ones.

Mary opened up the loft, talking to the birds, urging them to fly. A few came out. She didn't stay to see them all go, but ran indoors behind Phyl and Lennie.

Mum said, "I thought you'd want your supper before messing with those birds."

She had put out bowls of soup and was checking the potatoes in the oven. The heat from the fire reddened her face.

Baby Doreen was whimpering. Phyl picked her up and shushed her.

"Get your soup, Phyl," said Mum. "I'll take care of Doreen."

"Aren't you having any?" Phyl asked. The girls knew that sometimes their mother missed meals to save money. She had always been thin, but now the scraped-back hair revealed hollows under her cheekbones.

"I'll wait for your dad," she said.

They turned to the food, and there was silence, except for Lennie's slurping and an occasional hiccup from Doreen.

The potatoes had been cooked in the slow oven. They were soft, so that the skins just broke. Mary ate hers and scraped the plate. She felt she could have eaten ten more.

"If you're still hungry," said their mother, "there's bread and jam. But go easy on the bread."

Guiltily they spread jam on slices of bread and wolfed it down. Their mother went off to feed and change Doreen, and Phyl collected the dishes and fetched water from the shared tap in the yard.

Mary went back to the pigeons.

There were eight breeding pairs in the loft, ranging in age from the Gaffer down to the yearlings. The flock was circling overhead. Mary counted eight birds. Good. That meant the cocks were still sitting, and all the hens were out.

Mary loved to watch them. She heard the whir of their wings as they flew overhead. They passed behind the chimneys of the houses opposite and over toward Springhill Pit, where Dad had worked until it closed last year. The sun came out from behind a cloud and caught their light undersides and they all flashed together as they cornered and swung back.

They were beautiful. A team. And separately they were good, too. Ruby, named for her dark red eyes, was a strong little bird, had plenty of stamina, and never gave up; Lavender had won from Exeter last year. But there was one in particular that Dad had great hopes for: Speedwell. Speedwell was destined for Rennes, Nantes, maybe Bordeaux. There were other good racers in the loft: Bevin and True Blue had won short-distance races last year. But Speedwell was a granddaughter of the Gaffer, a long-distance racer. She was the one he would send to the south of France.

It had begun to rain while Mary stood watching the birds: a drizzle at first, then heavy soaking drops. Vaguely, above the sound of the rain and the cooing from the loft, she became aware of her own name— "Mary! MARY!" —shouted in increasing exasperation.

Mum was standing at the back door, Doreen screaming in the crook of her arm. With her free hand she held the laundry basket. Mary ran up the path.

"Get the laundry, for heaven's sake!" snapped Mum. She thrust the basket at Mary. "Couldn't you have grabbed it when it started to rain? Standing there gaping at those birds. You never think."

She went in, slamming the door.

Mary snatched clothespins from the line, tossing the clothes unfolded into the basket. They had been damp anyway, but they were getting rapidly wetter as she worked her way along. The rain soaked into the shoulders of her cardigan and trickled down the back of her neck.

With the line cleared, she backed in through the door with the heavy basket. Her mother was ironing.

"Hang them around the fire," she said.

Mary began draping towels and diapers over the rack.

"You never think," said Mum again. "There's Phyl putting Lennie to bed, and I had Doreen, and what are you doing? Standing out in the rain staring up at those damn pigeons."

She banged the iron down, folded a pillowcase, and picked up a blouse.

Mary hung the last diaper on the rack.

"I have to shut them away," she said.

"Yes, and when you've done that you can take these things upstairs," said Mum.

Mary went to the door.

"The laundry was wet, anyway," she said, and

flounced out before her mother could answer. She was angry because she knew she should have noticed; somehow she could never do anything right for her mother.

The shower was over. Light glinted on the pigeons' wings. She filled the feeding can and shook it, whistling. They came at once, swooping down to the loft. She took a last look at the squeaker, then shut them in.

Back indoors, she had scooped up a pile of ironed clothes from the table and was on her way upstairs when familiar footsteps sounded in the passage. Dad was back!

She dumped the clothes on the top step and ran downstairs. Phyl followed her.

Dad closed the door and hung his coat on the hook. They could see from his face that he'd had no luck.

"Sit down, love," said Mum. "I'll warm the soup."

Dad sat in his chair by the fire.

"Nothing," he said.

Mary felt apprehensive. This voice and this slump of the shoulders were not like her father, not the Dad she knew. Dad was always so full of enthusiasm. She'd seen him standing up at union meetings, "sounding off," as Mum would call it, his voice ringing, his shoulders thrown back. And in the loft, with the pigeons, he was gentle—you had to be—but he was confident. He knew his system was right. He knew his pigeons were winners. And in any crisis he was always the one who knew what to do.

Mary, wanting to make things right again, said, "Dad, we've got a squeaker! Lavender and Lenin's. I found it when I got home. And Dad, the hens are flying so well—"

"Mary!" her mother exclaimed, swinging around on her. "Your dad's got more important things to think about than pigeons!"

But Dad's eyes had brightened, as Mary hoped they would. She shot her mother a look of triumph.

"That's good, Mary," said Dad. "I'll go down later."

Mum ladled out soup for herself and Dad—a few spoonfuls for her, a bowlful for him.

"What are we going to do?" she asked.

Chapter Two

Mary knelt on the mat by the fire, watching her mother and Phyl clearing the table and putting the dishes in the sink. All through the meal Mum had talked, in a low anxious voice, about the expenses they faced: shoes for Lennie and Phyl, medicine for Doreen's cough, the rent going up next month.

Dad still sat at the table. He hadn't said anything, but Mary guessed that he had come to a decision, even before he reached home. He stood up, scraping his chair on the floor, and everyone turned to look at him.

"I'll have to go and look for work," he said. "Up Stafford way. Plenty of pits there. I'm sure to find something. Then I can send money home."

"So it's come to that," Mum said.

"It won't be for long. Things are sure to pick up around here soon. We have a Labor government now."

"Labor!" Mum clattered the dishes in the sink. "The pit bosses will do what they want, Labor or no Labor."

"Things will change," said Dad. "It'll take time."

"They won't get time," said Mum. "They were out eight months last time. What good did that do?"

There was silence. They had had this argument before.

Then Mum said, "How will you live, while you're looking for work? Where will you sleep?"

"I'll find somewhere."

"Flophouses."

"Most likely, yes." He turned to the girls. "You must help your mother while I'm away."

Phyl said, "But, Dad, I'm going away, too, remember?"

Phyl was leaving home on Saturday and going to work as a maid at a big house out in the country eight miles away. It had all been arranged several months ago.

"I hadn't forgotten," said Mum. "Oh, Phyl, I'm glad you have a job, but I wish you'd gotten fixed up at the china factory or in a shop—something local. It would have been a help, to have you here."

Meaning I'm not a help, thought Mary.

There were times when Mary resented Phyl. Phyl was her mother's girl. She even looked like Mum: thin and quick moving, with straight dark hair and gray eyes. Phyl always managed to do the right thing, always noticed when the baby needed to be changed or the laundry brought in. She wrote neatly and could sew with neat fast stitches. Mary's sewing invariably ended up dirty, uneven, and spotted with blood. Mary had once overheard Mrs. Lloyd, next door, saying of Phyl, "She's a little treasure around the house, that one." She wondered what people said about her. They wouldn't call her a little treasure. They might say, "That Mary that's always around the pigeons" (disapprovingly, because girls weren't supposed to like pigeons) or, "That big dreamy lump—you'd never think she was Phyl Dyer's sister."

Mary said, in an aggrieved tone, "I can help."

Mum looked at her. "You'll certainly need to shape up once Phyl's gone."

Mary glowered.

Her mother sat down and began unpicking the hem of a dress. It wasn't her own; she did alterations and mending to earn a few extra shillings.

"Leave that now, Lina," Dad said.

"I can't. Mrs. Miller wants it tomorrow."

Dad looked irritated. Mary knew he hated her having to work.

"Well, Mary," he said, "let's go and see that squeaker, shall we?"

Much later, when Mary and Phyl were upstairs in

20

bed, they heard their parents talking, the talk rising to an argument. The voices were sometimes clear, sometimes muffled, as they moved between the two downstairs rooms.

Phyl sat up. "Listen," she said.

But Mary couldn't catch the words, only the feel of what they meant: her mother's voice, sharp, accusing, her father's defensive rumble.

Phyl got out of bed and padded barefoot to the stairs. Reluctantly Mary followed her. She didn't like to hear her parents arguing, but Phyl never wanted to miss anything; she had to know.

Phyl was crouched on the bend of the stairs, just out of sight of the kitchen.

"And how long?" came Mum's voice. "How long will this go on?"

"I don't know, Lina. I don't want it any more than you do."

"That union," said Mum, spitting the word out like a swearword. "If only you'd stayed out of it."

"We're all in the union, Lina."

"Not like you!" she retorted. "Running things, speaking out, organizing. They won't forgive you for that, Tom."

Oh, Mum, leave him alone, thought Mary.

"It was a time to speak out," said Dad.

"But not—not always at the front of things. A ringleader. Your picture in the papers ..." Her voice cracked as if she were on the brink of tears.

Mary glanced up at the picture on the wall at the top of the stairs. It was a newspaper photograph, yellowing now, but preserved in a glass-fronted frame. It showed a group of miners outside the pit. Several held banners. The biggest banner read: NOT A MINUTE ON THE DAY: NOT A PENNY OFF THE PAY. One of the men holding it up was Dad. Underneath was a date: 4th May 1926. Four years ago, almost to the day. But now that pits were closing and work was scarce, the bosses hadn't forgotten the General Strike, nor who the local leaders had been. Most of the men laid off in Culverton last year had found work in other pits, but not Dad.

The voices became indistinct again. And then came the sound of someone stoking the fire. That meant they were coming to bed. Mary tugged at Phyl's arm. Phyl strained to hear more, but when the voices drew closer to the stairs she gave in to Mary and they scuttled back to bed.

Neither could sleep. They whispered for a while, till Dad called out from across the landing. "Go to sleep, you girls." They each lay silent with her thoughts.

Mary wondered what it would be like at home without Dad or Phyl, just Mum and the little ones. She was always in trouble with Mum over one thing or another, but Phyl would cover up for her and defend her. She'd miss Phyl. And Dad. She'd enjoyed the time he had been off work; they'd spent a lot of it in the loft, taking care of the pigeons.

Well, we have a few more days all together, she thought.

But Saturday soon came. Phyl was up early, too nervous to eat breakfast. She pulled back her hair into a knot on the nape of her neck and put on a dress of dark blue cotton with a white collar and a pin-tucked front. Auntie Elsie, Dad's sister, had made her two dark blue dresses and two white aprons and had found her a hat with cherries on it and trimmed it with a blue ribbon.

Mary sniffed the new cotton of the dress. She was jealous. She'd never had a dress that wasn't an old one of Phyl's with the waist let out, or one of Auntie Elsie's cut down. And the hat! Phyl put it on and was transformed into a grown-up.

Mary said, "Oh, Phyl! Can I try it?"

She took the hat and darted into her parents' room to look at herself in the flecked mirror.

Mary's face was rounder than Phyl's, and her hair was a lighter brown and sprang about in curls. The hat hovered on top of them.

"It's too small," said Mary. But the ribbon was silky, and the cherries trembled as she turned her head. She felt beautiful.

Phyl took it back and minced around the room.

Mary put on a gentrified voice: "Phyllis! Bring in

23

the tea things!''

They both giggled. ''Fat chance!'' said Phyl. ''I'll be scrubbing the passage, probably.''

Mum called up the stairs, ''Phyl! Come and eat something, love. You'll be an hour on that bus.''

At ten o'clock they were all at the bus stop in the square: Dad, Mary holding Lennie's hand, Mum carrying Doreen wrapped in a shawl, and Phyl holding a brown paper bag of spare clothes and a purse with her bus fare in it.

Her employers had sent the bus fare with a letter saying that someone would meet her at the bus stop at Wendon. Dad would have liked to go too, to make sure she arrived safely, but there was no money to spare for the journey.

The bus was already quite full when it arrived. Dad took Phyl's paper bag and settled her in a seat, and then they all watched and waved as the bus pulled away and Phyl craned to look back.

Mum was a little weepy, and Mary felt tears coming too. She wouldn't see Phyl for at least a month; Phyl would get every other Sunday off, but she wouldn't want to squander her wages on coming home every time.

And tomorrow Dad was going, and no one knew for how long.

That evening Dad went to the pigeon loft with Mary to say goodbye to his birds. A deep, soft, comfortable

24

cooing came from within as they approached.

"I'll miss that sound," said Dad.

He went along the row, talking to all the birds. The Gaffer flew down and perched on his shoulder.

Monday's squeaker was growing big, and Lavender's other egg had hatched.

"Number Fifty-eight's will be next," said Dad, pointing out a sitting hen.

"Queenie's," said Mary.

"Queenie. That's right." Dad smiled.

Dad would never have bothered with names if it hadn't been for Mary. Mary insisted that the birds should all have names as well as numbers. When she asked Dad to choose names his mind went to politics, as usual—to his favorite political figures, his heroes. So they had Bevin and Lenin and Ramsay Mac and Mrs. Pankhurst. Mary thought Dad's names were silly; she liked to choose a name that suited each bird. She was especially pleased with Speedwell, the blue checker hen whose name had a double meaning: the blue of the speedwell flowers that grew wild in the garden, and the hope that the bird would fly fast.

Dad was handling Speedwell now, stretching out her wing with its long, dark-tipped feathers.

"She's a lovely bird," he said. "Lovely condition. I wish I could be here to race her this summer."

"I can race her," said Mary.

"No. We'll just have to miss a year."

"We won't!" exclaimed Mary, startling the Gaffer, who flew up onto a high perch. "I can race her, Dad! I know how. And Uncle Charley would help me."

"Oh, he would," agreed Dad. "But it's a big job, Mary, studying the birds, working out which ones are on form, and which one to send where, and when. It'll be enough for me if you just take good care of them—keep them exercised."

Mary felt hurt. Why didn't he believe she could do it?

"It'll be a waste," she said, "if she doesn't race this summer."

"There's always another race, another year," said Dad.

Another year. That sounded like eternity to Mary. They said no more about it, but Mary had made up her mind: she was going to take care of the birds and race them. Dad would be proud of her. Even Mum would, if she got some winnings. She visualized the coming summer as a pale blue line growing bluer through May and June till it reached a deep sapphire color in late July. And in the midst of that deep blue was a place she knew only from maps and her imagination: the south of France.

Chapter Three

"You're bursting out of that dress already," said Mum. "I'm sure I was never that big at eleven."

"I'm almost twelve," said Mary.

"Pity you're not twelve yet."

Mum was thinking of money. At twelve Mary would be able to get a part-time job—an hour after school helping in a shop. Phyl had helped at the fabric shop. She had sold elastic, ribbons, and pins, but she hadn't been allowed to cut lengths of cloth.

"Don't you want to?" Mary had asked, picturing Mrs. Coleman's scissors shearing through the width of the material; rayon was the best: a swift, swishing cut. "I'd want to cut cloth."

Phyl had shrugged, not understanding the question. She wasn't allowed to, and that was that.

Mary thought she'd like to do a delivery round: milk

or groceries. But it was always the boys who got those jobs. The bicycles they used were designed for boys, with a straight crossbar that was awkward if you wore a skirt.

Dad had a bike like that, with a basket in front like a delivery boy's. He used it for taking the pigeons on training tosses, and when Mary was smaller she had often gone with him, sitting in front on the crossbar, bumping along the lanes, past pits and quarries and spoil heaps, out to the countryside.

I'll get the birds out there somehow, thought Mary, *if I have to walk.* You could send them by train, but that wasn't the same. When you took them yourself you had a sense of how far they had flown. She remembered the bright air, the big sky, the fields stretching out, the quiet; and then the rush of wings as the pigeons took off, circled a few times, and made for home.

Dad had gone on his bike to Stafford. He had taken True Blue with him in a basket and released the bird when he arrived; he had no money for postage stamps, and True Blue was quicker. So they knew Dad had arrived safely, but they had heard nothing since—not for almost three weeks.

"He'd have to find a job," said Mum, "then work a week before getting paid, and then it'll be a day or two, won't it, getting the money order and sending it? I wonder if that maroon one Auntie Elsie gave us would do for you?"

Mary was used to her mother's thought processes. They were back to Mary and the too-small dress. Mary remembered the maroon dress and winced. It was dark and droopy, with an old-ladyish look about it.

Mum whipped out a tape measure. "Hold out your arm. Stand still ... You know, it might do. Cut down." She tut-tutted. "You've got your Auntie Elsie's figure, and no mistake."

Mary visualized Auntie Elsie. Her figure was not much in evidence, since she usually wore shapeless cardigans over skirts that had not yet risen to the fashionable shorter lengths. But there was an impression of solid bosom, thick waist, and sturdy legs. Very different from Mum.

She looked across at a photograph on the mantelpiece. It showed Mary's mother as a young woman: a studio portrait with a backdrop of painted trees. Her mother wore a high-necked lacy blouse and a long narrow skirt, and she carried a parasol. A hat with roses on it was balanced on top of her piled dark hair. At the bottom of the photograph was her name, neatly printed: Miss Adeline Hill.

Mary had always loved that photograph. Her mother was so slim and pretty, and Mary had dreamed of one day looking like her. Phyl would, of course— she'd seen that look in Phyl when she pulled back her hair and put on the hat with the cherries. *But not me,* she realized now. *I'll never look like Mum. I'll look like Auntie Elsie.*

She turned to her mother. "You don't like Auntie Elsie, do you?"

"What?" Her mother blushed, startled. "Don't be silly. You know how good she's always been to us."

She put the tape measure away.

"Now, I want you to go to Greening's and get some groceries. I'll write a list and you can go to the fabric shop and see if you can get some dark sewing cotton for that dress. Don't bother matching it. Black or brown will do."

Resignation crept over Mary. Saturday was Mum's cleaning day and that always meant extra chores for Mary: do the shopping, hang the laundry, peel the potatoes, mind Doreen, mind Lennie. She'd be lucky to find much time for the pigeons today. Still, shopping was better than helping with the cleaning.

"And can you pop in and see Uncle Charley? He might need something."

Mary went to see Uncle Charley first. She liked him. He was her mother's uncle, retired long ago from the pit with dust on the lungs. He couldn't get around much, although he managed to creep the few yards to the Rose and Crown every night. Dad often met him there. The pub had a meeting room at the back where the pigeon club met. Dad and Uncle Charley both went to the meetings, although Charley didn't race anymore; he just kept a few old favorites.

They were soon out in the garden, looking at the pigeons and the few chickens that were scratching around among the nettles. Uncle Charley found four eggs and gave them to Mary to take home.

"All of them?" asked Mary.

"One each."

"Doreen doesn't eat regular food yet."

"Well, two for your mum, then."

"Mum wouldn't eat two."

"She should. Tell her."

"But she won't. And what about you?"

Uncle Charley laughed. The laugh turned into a cough, and he coughed and coughed; his face was gray. When he got his breath back, he said, "Don't worry about me. A pot of tea and some bread and jam. That'll do for me. Now, tell me about your pigeons. Nice flying weather. Are you training them?"

Mary pulled a face. "Trying to. I want to take them out on a toss. Not just a mile or two—I've done that—but a real one, five miles, or seven, out in the country. But there's never any time. It's school all week, and then after school and on Saturdays Mum says do this, do that, and I don't get a minute."

"Well, you must help your mother."

"I know, but . . ."

Mary paused. An idea was forming in her mind, but she didn't dare tell Uncle Charley about it. He'd be

31

shocked. She was a little shocked herself. She changed the subject.

"Dad thinks Speedwell's a winner. Best long-distance bird he's had. I want to put her in for Bordeaux in July."

"Bordeaux! That's over seven hundred miles, girl."

"She could do it. She won last year from Nevers, didn't she?"

"That's true, she did. She's a lovely bird. Try her on four hundred-odd later this month. There's Le Mans, or Nantes. I'll put her in for you."

"Thank you." Mary wished she could go to the club herself, but Mum had forbidden it. The pigeon club was a man's place, she said; she didn't want Mary hanging around a public house; besides, there was enough for her to do at home.

"But the races," Mary had protested.

"Your father asked you to look after them, not race them."

"But that is looking after them!" Mary exclaimed. "I might win some money," she added.

"And you might lose some. You'll get no money for pools from me."

"Dad puts them in. He pools them," said Mary.

"Yes." Her mother was tightlipped. "What a pity. But I decide where the money goes now, and it doesn't go on pigeons. If your Uncle Charley's daft enough to put them in for you, that's his affair."

Uncle Charley was daft enough.

"I'll find out the dates for you—tell you what's best," he promised.

He put the four dirt-spattered precious eggs into a paper bag. Mary took it straight home, for fear of breaking them.

"Oh, bless him!" said Mum, and her face softened with relief and gratitude. "I didn't know what we were going to eat today. You know, Mary, if that money order doesn't come on Monday we'll have to go to the Public Assistance Committee and ask for help. Now go and get that shopping done."

Mary went, her mind full of her audacious plan.

Chapter Four

Mary woke up early on Sunday morning, as she had planned. She sat up, willing the bed springs not to squeak. The bed was an old double one with a lumpy mattress. Mary had slept on one side of it; she still could not get used to having all that space to herself. The room faced east and was full of sunlight. It was going to be a beautiful day—too good to spend in chapel.

Mary slid her feet out onto the cool cracked linoleum and began putting on her clothes. From behind the screen, which gave her the illusion of being in a room of her own, Lennie was snoring gently.

The window was in Mary's half of the room. She looked out. Behind the roofs of the houses opposite rose the headframe of the pit; the sunlight sparkled and she had to squint to see, over to the left, pit mounds and scarred earth giving way in the distance to green hills. That was where she was going: right out of Culverton with its pits and brickworks and streets into the distant, green countryside.

With her shoes in her hand she crept past Lennie, flat on his back with mouth open and arms flung up, onto the landing, past the closed door of the room where Mum and Doreen slept, and downstairs.

In the kitchen she got a drink of water. Then she cut two thick slices of bread and wrapped them in a paper bag. She found an empty vinegar bottle and filled it with water. Under the teapot she pushed the note she had written last night.

Outside the back door, she looked up at Mum's window. There was no sound, and the curtain was drawn. Mum wouldn't wake easily; she liked to sleep late on Sundays.

The pigeons, on the other hand, were wide awake, all glossy feathers and gleaming eyes. There was one she noticed particularly as she handled the young birds: a dark checker cock with a bold eye; he sat beautifully balanced in her hands.

Mary gave the birds a drink and got out the basket. She put in six of the young birds, those that had hatched that spring. She thought about taking some of the yearlings, too, to help keep the flock together, but when she lifted the basket she knew that six was plenty. Besides, Uncle Charley had come by last night with the race dates and had promised to put some birds on the train to Gloucester on Tuesday, to give them a longer run.

Mary put her food and vinegar bottle in the pockets of her dress, heaved up the basket, and went out through the back garden gate.

It was not until she reached the end of Lion Street that she began to think about the consequences of what she was doing.

No decent person flew pigeons on a Sunday. Sunday racing was forbidden. Even Sunday visits to friends' lofts were frowned upon; and Mary's place on a Sunday was at chapel in the morning and at Auntie Elsie's for tea in the afternoon. She'd be in trouble, for certain, when she got home.

She should have asked, she thought; but then, justifying herself, if she had asked, Mum would have said no. There would be trouble, but it seemed to Mary that she could not avoid it, since the young birds needed a toss and she was determined to be the one to take them. Anyway, at this early hour, the afternoon and its retribution seemed a long way off. She was more concerned now about the weight of the basket and the way it scraped and bumped into her leg. She stopped and changed hands.

The rows of terraced houses began to thin out and she found herself trudging along a lane of rutted earth with only an occasional cottage here and there. The headframe of Old Hall Pit came in sight to her left, and the spoil heaps rose all around, blocking the view.

Mary stopped by a stile, put down the heavy basket, and ate one of the slices of bread. The pigeons shuffled in the basket and cooed softly. The mine was motionless in the Sunday silence, and from the cottages there was no sign of life except a cat that was eyeing her from the top of a wall. Maybe its ears had caught the sounds from the pigeon basket.

"You keep away, cat," said Mary. She didn't like cats; they were always prowling around the loft.

She climbed over the stile and walked on. She was getting tired; the basket was too heavy. But gradually the pit mounds were giving way to fields and hedgerows. The air was clearer and there was a scent of flowers.

When she stopped at midday she was surrounded by fields; all she could see of Culverton was a distant church spire. She put down the basket and sat on a stile, then ate the second slice of bread and drank the water.

Young green wheat was growing in the field on one side of the stile and clover on the other. Beyond a hedge was some bright green crop that she couldn't recognize at this distance. Far away, across several fields, there was a line of people bending, weeding. There was no sound except the rustle of wheat and, high up, the faint summery sounds of skylarks calling.

"Time to go," said Mary to the birds. She got down from the stile and began unfastening the straps on the basket. The pigeons fluttered and cooed. They were hungry now, eager to get home; she hadn't fed them this morning. They ought to be all right, but she was nervous. You could never be sure with young birds, and they hadn't been taken this far from home before.

The lid was down; a couple of birds ventured out. For a second or two they stayed. When one, the bold-looking dark checker cock, took off, the others came out and followed with a whir of wings, and Mary knew it was out of her hands now; they were away. They circled around for several minutes, not as smoothly as her flock of older hens, but connected, moving as a group. Then, suddenly, they veered off. They were heading home. Mary felt both relief and apprehension. Her one desire now was to return home herself and be sure that they all got back safely. She bent to fasten the basket.

When she looked up again the birds had vanished. And then she saw one dropping down toward the field beyond the hedge.

"Oh, no—you mustn't!" Mary was panic-stricken. If they stopped to feed they might never go home. She'd have to chase them off.

She seized the basket and ran awkwardly with it along the edge of the field and over the next stile. They were all down. What was it, that bright green? Of course. Peas. Young peas—the first crop almost ready for harvesting. Pigeons couldn't resist them. If only she'd noticed; Dad would have.

She jumped down from the stile, and as she did so a gunshot rang out, followed by a rush of wings. A man had appeared at the bottom of the field. Pigeons were circling above in panic. Had he gotten one? Mary couldn't see. The gun was pointed skyward again.

"No!" screamed Mary. "No!"

The man fired again, and the flock scattered.

Mary ran down the side of the field, yelling, "No! Don't shoot! They're going! Look, they're going away!"

The man ignored her. He aimed and fired a third time. Mary saw a pigeon plummet.

She threw herself at the man.

"You didn't have to kill it! It was flying away! You only had to scare them off. Why did you kill it?"

The man lowered the gun and turned to her. She quailed at the sight of his anger.

"Because dead pigeons don't come back," he said. "I'll shoot every one I see. You people with your damned pigeons are a menace."

"I didn't know," said Mary, sniffing back tears. "I didn't realize it was peas."

She started forward to retrieve her dead pigeon, but the man caught her arm and flung her back.

"Off my land, miss!"

"I want my pigeon!"

The man's face darkened. "Just get off my land. Get off! Go! And don't come back!"

Mary backed away, terrified. The man looked so angry she feared he might turn the gun on her. She ran back to the stile, grabbed her basket, and climbed over into the next field, out of his sight. She ran, gasping for breath, until she reached a gate with a stile in it and knew she was on the footpath that would lead her home.

She stopped then, put down the basket, and stared up at the sky. They had all gone. But had they gone home or were they scattered? They had been frightened and might lose their bearings. Once they were separated they could be picked up by other flocks. And then there were hawks, and telegraph wires, and, if they came down, cats. It was miles home to find out if they were safe, and Mum was going to be so angry, and if she'd lost the pigeons then Dad had lost all his new season's birds.

"That bloody farmer!" said Mary. She beat her fist on the gate and began to cry in earnest, hating the farmer, hating herself for being so stupid, hating the thought of going home.

She was not aware of anyone's approach until a voice behind her said, "What's up with you, then, Mary Dyer?"

Mary looked around, trying to control the

trembling of her chin. She saw a boy—a rough-looking boy, dark-haired and dark-eyed, with a bruise on one cheekbone and an air rifle over his shoulder. He was swarthy with a darkness that was more dirt than nature and he wore a ragged shirt and trousers and shoes that had split open at the sides.

Arnold Revell. Just about the last person Mary would have wanted to meet.

Chapter Five

All the girls shrank from Arnold Revell.

"He smells," Doris Brown would say, wrinkling her little nose. And it was true that a fusty, unwashed odor, sometimes mixed with a rank smell of goat, emanated from the corner where Arnold sat at the back of the class. His nails were usually black and his neck grimy. He was not exactly badly behaved, but school didn't interest him and he brought an air of disorder into the classroom. Farther down the school were more Revells. Almost every class had one. Arnold was the oldest. He had been kept back at least a year because he was so slow, and he was bigger and older than everyone else in his class. The Revells lived on an allotment and scrapyard on the edge of town out beyond the railway station. Whenever there was petty thieving, apple stealing, or fights, the Revells were blamed.

Mary sniffed back her tears and steadied her chin. She didn't want to cry in front of Arnold Revell. Had it been Olive, or, better still, Phyl, she would have burst into tears again and enjoyed their sympathy. But not a boy, especially this boy.

"I heard shooting," said Arnold. He looked at the pigeon basket. "Someone shoot your birds?"

"Yes," said Mary. She picked up the basket, but it seemed rude to turn her back on him and go, so she explained about the peas and how angry the farmer had been.

"I heard the shooting and dived into the hedge," said Arnold. "Best keep out of the way, I thought. I don't get along with farmers, see.

"Course, if I'd known it was you," he added gallantly, "I'd have come out and had a go at the bugger."

Mary thought it was just as well he hadn't.

She began climbing over the stile, hampered by the basket. Arnold took it from her, then swung himself over with practiced ease. Mary thought how much better he fitted into the countryside than he did into the classroom. There, he looked stupid and clumsy; here, he seemed to belong.

"Going home?" asked Arnold.

"Yes." Mary didn't want him walking along beside her, but the footpath was bordered by hedges and there was nowhere else to go.

"What were you doing back there?" she asked.

Arnold shrugged. "Nothing much. Looking around. Get a few rabbits sometimes."

The thought of meat made Mary aware of how hungry she was.

"How many of your pigeons got shot?" asked Arnold.

"One, at least. Maybe two."

"Pity he stopped you getting them. Makes a good meal, a couple of pigeons. Nice with a bit of gravy."

Mary wondered how many racing pigeons Arnold had shot in his time; she doubted whether he would make much distinction between ringed ones and wild ones.

"Mum might have forgiven me if I'd brought them back," she agreed. She explained to Arnold what she had done. Arnold did not seem shocked about the Sunday flying or about not going to chapel; the Revells rarely attended, and when they did nobody sat near them.

"I'm scared to go home," confessed Mary.

"Come to our place, then. Got some stew. Chicken."

"Wouldn't your mum mind?"

"Mum? She took off again. There's only Dad and the little uns."

Mary thought of chicken stew and was tempted.

After all, Arnold seemed all right. But the Revells had such a bad reputation in town; she wasn't sure she ought to go there. And if Mum found out ... *I'm in enough trouble already*, Mary thought. Besides, there were the pigeons; she had to see if they had gotten home.

"I'd better not," she said.

It took them over an hour to walk back to Culverton, but the time passed quickly. Arnold told Mary about scrapes he and his brothers had gotten into. They involved mostly air rifles, trespassing, or thieving. Mary was mildly shocked, but the stories made her laugh; she suspected that her laughter was making Arnold exaggerate them. Then they entered the fringe of town, and Mary stopped laughing and chatting and began to worry. First, she worried about the time. Mum and the little ones should have gone up to Auntie Elsie's by now, but they might be waiting for her at home. Then she worried about being seen with Arnold. It was bad enough being seen with any boy—the girls always teased one another—but Arnold Revell: she'd never live it down if anyone saw her with him.

They came to the parting of the ways: Lion Street for Mary and Station Road for Arnold. Mary paused.

"I've got to go now."

Arnold was still carrying the pigeon basket. She reached for it.

"Heavy, after a few miles, that is," said Arnold, handing it back.

"You didn't have to carry it," said Mary ungraciously.

"I meant for you. With pigeons in. You need a bike."

Mary laughed. "Fat chance!"

"See you, then. Tomorrow."

"See you."

Mary turned away and ran up Lion Street. Tomorrow! She hoped he wouldn't speak to her tomorrow at school. She'd die.

She went along the alley and in through the back garden gate. Now her thoughts were all for the pigeons. She wanted to fling open the door of the loft and rush inside, but she restrained herself and approached it calmly so as not to disturb the birds.

Three of them were back. Three out of six. Two had probably been shot. One was lost; it might find its way back, but it was young and the outside world was full of dangers. The beautiful dark checker cock was missing. Had he been shot? She'd never know which one it was she saw fall. She imagined him stiffening in the field of peas, his bloom gone, his bold red eye dulled.

Sorry, Dad, she thought.

Indoors, the house was empty. They hadn't waited. Auntie Elsie would be setting the table now, with the pretty plates painted with birds and flowers—seconds that Uncle Arthur used to bring home from the china factory. There would be sandwiches, and currant cake, and a small bag of sweets for Lennie. Mary felt almost sick with hunger. If she went up there now she'd be in time for tea. But it meant walking in, feeling everyone staring at her, confronting the anger of both women ... she couldn't face it. *I should have gone to Arnold's,* she thought. *Who cares what anyone thinks?*

She searched the pantry, found a crust of bread, and spread it with jam. Then she went up to her room to await her mother's anger.

Chapter Six

Mary's mother was angry. What would the neighbors think, she asked? What would the minister think? How did she think Auntie Elsie felt? Mary became aware that her mother had been subjected to an afternoon-long lecture by Auntie Elsie on how to discipline her children. "And on top of all that, I was worried the whole time. Didn't you realize I'd worry?"

Mary was sorry, but she wouldn't say so. "It's the only time I get, Sundays," she muttered, hanging her head.

"You won't take those birds out on a Sunday again," said her mother.

Mary decided not to mention Arnold Revell. However, she told her mother about the shooting. She was hoping for sympathy, but got none.

"You can't blame the farmer. He's got his crops to protect. He's probably driven crazy by pigeon fanciers. I know I am. And if you think I'm letting you off on Saturdays, you can think agin. I won't have a girl your age running around the countryside when she ought to be helping at home."

"Well, I'm sending three birds to Le Mans on Wednesday," said Mary defiantly. "If they win us some money you'll be pleased, won't you?"

"If," said Mum.

But the next morning everything was changed. The mailman came, bringing a letter from Dad. Mary and Lennie watched as Mum tore it open. Inside was a money order for four pounds, a one-shilling coin, and a letter.

"Four pounds!" Mum scanned the letter quickly. "That's two weeks' pay ... he's got a job ... temporary, but he'll keep looking around ... he'll send more next week. He says, 'Mary, the shilling is for pigeon feed.' He doesn't say where he's sleeping. I hope it's somewhere decent."

She stood holding the money order and staring at it as if afraid it would disappear.

Suddenly she laughed and hugged both children to her. "We'll have fish and chips tonight, okay? Here, take your shilling, Mary, for the pigeons. Don't lose it."

Mary took the shilling and quickly put it in her

pocket. She had half expected Mum to keep it, but the money order had made her generous. That, and Phyl coming next weekend. It was her Sunday off, and she would bring her wages.

Mary went to school. To her relief, Arnold Revell ignored her, not even catching her eye. When she got home there was a warm, greasy fish-and-chip smell in the kitchen. What was more, Mum had bought an orange. She gave it to Lennie and Mary to share. Mary broke her half into segments and ate it slowly, savoring the sharp, fresh taste. She pushed half the pieces to one side and said to her mother, "You have some."

Mum shook her head.

"Go on," insisted Mary.

"All right, just one." Mum took one segment.

Mary ate the others with a guilty feeling of relief.

Mum smiled. "I've finished that dress. You can try it on after tea."

Mary had to admit, standing in her mother's bedroom in front of the mirror, that the dress fit her; and it was more comfortable under the arms than the old, tight one. But the old one had been blue-flowered cotton and she had felt pretty in it. She hated this one: the dark plain color, the crepey material.

Mum stood up from where she had been adjusting the hem. She looked doubtful. "What do you think?"

"It's sort of floppy," said Mary, trying not to be

too discouraging, since her mother had spent time altering it.

"It doesn't flatter you," Mum admitted. She sighed. "But it fits. It'll have to do."

The maroon dress was the first bad thing that happened that week. The second was Arnold Revell speaking to her at school.

It was during the last break time on Wednesday. Mary was leaning against the wall in the playground with Olive, watching a skipping game and sucking a sherbet lemon. She had just bitten through the crisp shell of the lemon when she felt Olive nudge her. Arnold Revell was coming across the playground, heading straight toward them.

He stopped in front of Mary.

"Come by our place tonight," he said. "Got something to show you."

Then he turned away.

Olive exploded with laughter, spraying the scent of lemon around. "Hey, Mary, was he talking to you?"

"I don't know!" Mary exclaimed. She staggered against Olive, giggling, desperate to convince her friend that she had never spoken to Arnold before.

Arnold must have heard them, but he gave no sign. He just walked away.

Olive called to Doris Brown and Edna Johnson, who were standing nearby. "Did you hear that? Arnold Revell asked Mary out!"

"He didn't," insisted Mary, as Doris shrieked with laughter. The girls began exclaiming about the cheek of boys in general and of Arnold Revell in particular. Mary joined in.

Afterward, sitting in the classroom, she glanced at Arnold and felt ashamed. But he shouldn't have spoken to her, she thought, defending her betrayal; especially not in front of the other girls. And it was only then that she wondered, *What does he want to show me, anyway?*

Mary didn't go to the Revells after school. She went home, had her tea, then hurried to the loft to get Blériot, Thunder, and Speedwell ready for the race. First, she would take them to Uncle Charley's. He had promised to take them to the club to have the race rings put on and the clock set, ready for Mary to meet the train at five-thirty.

Mary thought Uncle Charley would approve of her choices. The birds were as bright and buoyant as she'd ever seen them. The two cocks both had squeakers to fly home to. Speedwell didn't, but Mary felt sure she would do well; she remembered how certain Dad had been about her. "I just have a feeling about that bird, Mary. I think she'll turn out to be the best long-distance bird I've had."

Mary stood still in the loft, watching the pigeons. The Gaffer was on the floor. He tugged at her shoelace. Mary picked up Speedwell. The hen sat calmly in her palm, rounded and warm. Her deep red eye was unafraid. Soon Speedwell would be flying back from Le Mans, over five hundred miles. How would she do it? How would she know the way?

"It's a mystery," Dad had said. "Some sort of sixth sense. Something we humans lost, or never had. See, they're creatures of the air, Mary. The air isn't just a blank space to them. It's as full of messages to them as Culverton High Street is to you."

"Do you ever think of them, when you're down in the pit?" Mary had asked. "Do you think of them up above you in the air?"

Dad had laughed. "No time down there for day-dreaming about pigeons. But when I come up, and see the sky again, yes, I think about them then. I can't wait to go and let them out—see them fly. Sometimes I wish I were one. We've had our wings clipped, us working folk. But not you, Mary. Not yet. Get yourself an education. Get some learning. You could still fly."

Mary hadn't been sure what he was talking about. But the mention of education had suggested a lecture coming on, so she'd sidled away and begun refilling the water containers.

Now, Speedwell struggled against Mary's enclosing hand. Mary put the bird down. Speedwell stepped delicately off Mary's hand into her nest box. Mary watched, admiring the line of her: the strong deep chest curve, swooping up to the slim neck and intelligent head.

"We'll show them, won't we, Speedwell?" she said.

Just before five-thirty Mary was waiting at the railway station, carrying her empty pigeon basket. Her three birds had been taken to the Rose and Crown and put into one of the big club baskets, which now stood stacked on the platform. The baskets were surrounded by pigeon fanciers, all men or boys. Mostly they were miners or people from the china factory or the iron foundry; but the doctor was there, too, a young man standing a little apart from the others, who jostled and called to each other, "All right, Joe?" "All right, Len," and talked animatedly of form and eye-sign and training methods.

Like the doctor, Mary felt an outsider. Uncle Charley hadn't been able to come; his cough was bad. A few of the men, friends of her father, came up and spoke to her and asked her about her birds. But she still felt strange, the only female and one of the youngest people there.

She was relieved when she heard the train coming and looked along the track to see steam rising in clouds above the treetops. She looked across at the baskets and saw flickerings of eyes and feathers through the gaps. There was no telling which birds were hers.

The train pulled into the station and halted with a

a hissing sigh. Everyone began moving toward the guard's van. One by one the baskets were lifted and loaded in. Silently Mary wished the racers luck. *Fly well, Speedwell. Fly well, all of you.*

The door was slammed shut, the station master blew his whistle, and the train gathered steam and began moving slowly away.

They were gone. Gone to the coast, then across the sea to France. Mary had found Le Mans on the map of Europe that Dad kept in the drawer of the dresser. Le Mans was over four hundred miles away. The birds would not be released before Saturday morning, and only then if the weather was right; she could not hope to see Speedwell again before Sunday. Not unless she flew like the wind—or like Lady Marseilles. Mary remembered how excited Dad had been three years ago when they had all heard about Lady Marseilles. She had been released in Marseilles at ten-thirty in the morning and returned to her loft in Yorkshire at six o'clock on the evening of the next day. "Incredible," Dad had said. And, because he was a man who liked to keep notes of things, he'd written down the details on the edge of the map of Europe: "Seven hundred and eighty-eight miles at a velocity of nine hundred and thirty-nine yards per minute."

Mary dreamed of Speedwell becoming famous and gaining a new name: Lady Le Mans, or Lady Bordeaux. She saw certificates, silver cups on the mantelpiece, pictures in the *Racing Pigeon*. "Miss Dyer, owner of Lady Bordeaux." Only Speedwell wasn't hers, of course, she was Dad's. *But one day*, thought Mary, *I'll have pigeons of my own*.

The station was emptying. Mary turned away. It was all over now. The pigeons were gone, and she must wait till Sunday or even Monday to see them again. She'd go home now and Mum would have a stack of chores lined up for her. Washing the steps. Ironing. Cutting squares of newspaper for the toilet.

She had reached the top of the station approach. Lion Street lay to the left. To the right the road twisted and dwindled to a lane. At the end of the lane lay Sid Revell's allotment and scrapyard. Mary looked down the lane. She remembered what Arnold had said about having something to show her.

Whatever it was, it had to be more interesting than going straight home.

Chapter Seven

As she approached the Revells' home, Mary slowed
down. She was beginning to regret her decision. The
house was a dilapidated wooden bungalow surrounded by sheds and outhouses with corrugated iron roofs
and peeling paintwork. Heaps of scrap iron and rusty
machinery lay everywhere, and weeds grew waist-high
between the buildings. Two dogs, a ginger one and a
black one, lay sleeping, chained to their kennels. A
white nanny goat was tied to a post.

A line of grayish laundry, inexpertly pinned, hung
near the house. There was no sign of Arnold.

Mary was about to turn away when the ginger dog
woke. It leaped to its feet and began an outburst of
frenzied barking, straining at the chain. Another
volley of barking resounded from across the yard as
the black dog awoke.

It was too late to go now. A child's voice yelled, "Shut up, you two!" and Molly Revell—"snotty Molly," as she was known at school because of her constantly runny nose—came out of the bungalow and stared at Mary with her mouth open.

Mary didn't dare come closer because of the dogs. She shouted, "Is Arnold there?"

Molly yelled again at the dogs, "Shut up, will you?" To Mary she shouted, "They won't hurt you."

Mary noticed then that a man was strolling across from behind one of the heaps of scrap iron. Sid Revell. Mary half expected him to order her to clear out, but instead he stared at her briefly, then said, "Looking for Arnold?"

"Yes," said Mary.

Sid jerked his head. "He's down the field—behind those sheds. Don't mind Buster."

Mary looked at Buster, the ginger dog. His kennel was blocking her way.

"He won't hurt you," said Sid.

Mary edged past the kennel. Buster had found a well-gnawed bone. He sniffed at her skirt as she passed, then went back to cracking the bone with his back teeth.

Mary followed the path around behind the sheds and saw Arnold. He was in a field, riding a horse.

Mary leaned on the fence and watched. She was astonished. This boy, who seemed so clumsy and useless in school, was riding easily, gracefully.

Arnold saw her and dismounted. He came across the field, leading the horse, which shook its mane and blew soft breath into Mary's face.

"Thought you wouldn't come," said Arnold.

Mary shrugged and patted the horse's nose.

"Want to see?" Arnold vaulted over the fence to Mary's side.

"All right," she said, trying not to sound too interested. "I was just passing," she added. "I had to put some pigeons on the train."

"Where are they going?"

"Le Mans."

"Is that France?"

"Yes. It's more than four hundred miles back."

Arnold looked interested, unlike Mum or Phyl, and she found herself telling him about Speedwell and her hopes of winning. They walked back to the clutter of corrugated iron sheds.

"See, I got something for you," Arnold said.

Leaning against a wall, deep among the nettles, was a bicycle. It was rusty and bent. The saddle was split and the chain was missing. The handlebars were twisted at an awkward angle.

Arnold pulled the bicycle away from the wall.

"It's a woman's bike, see? About the right size for you. And this frame on the front"—he grabbed the pigeon basket that Mary was still carrying—"this'll take your basket."

The basket dropped obediently into position.

Mary understood. She felt hot with embarrassment. "We ... we don't have any money," she explained. "Dad's been out of work. I can't buy a bike—not even ..."

She looked doubtfully at the rusty machine.

"It's all right," said Arnold. "You can have it. I'll fix it up and you can have it. Never paid nothing for it, anyway. Found it in a ditch."

Best place for it, Mary thought. She didn't like to appear ungrateful, but it didn't look much good. And even if Arnold could fix it, as he said, should she accept it? She had a feeling her mother wouldn't approve. You didn't let people give you things, unless they were family. Or maybe neighbors. Not people like the Revells. She was sure her mother would not approve of the Revells' giving her things.

"I ought to pay for it," she said.

"Well ..." Arnold said, "there was something ..."

"What?"

"A couple of pigeons?"

Mary was shocked and hurt. "I thought you shot your own," she said coldly.

"No!" he exclaimed. "Not that! I mean a pair ... one of each, like"—he blushed under the dirt—"to breed from. I'd like to race them, see. The old man's not interested, but I like them. I like all animals."

"The thing is, they're not mine," said Mary. "And Dad's away."

"When he comes back, then?"

"I'll ask him."

"I'll do the bike anyway," said Arnold, turning to it as if he couldn't wait to get started. "Needs a new saddle and chain, bit of polishing up. The wheels are buckled but I can fix those. It'll be all right."

Mary thought of cycling out to a toss with the pigeons on the front. She could go twice—three times—as far. And then she thought of those delivery boys on their bikes, hogging all the best jobs. She'd have a chance now.

She smiled at Arnold. "Thanks," she said.

Mary didn't tell her mother about the bicycle, but she told Phyl. Phyl came home for the day on Sunday, startling them all with her new, short haircut.

"Annie, that I share a room with, she did it for me," said Phyl. "Annie says it's the latest thing."

"Well . . ." said Mum.

Phyl looked so different, rounder in the face, her eyes bigger.

Lennie hung back, shy of this new Phyl.

Phyl put her basket on the table. She had brought gifts. First, there was her wages, placed proudly in Mum's hand. Then, some fresh peas from the kitchen garden at Wendon Hall, wrapped in a brown paper bag. Finally, but best of all, four custard tarts from a batch baked in the Hall kitchen. The cook had slipped them into Phyl's basket.

Glad as she was to have Phyl home, Mary felt jealous. Mum was fussing over Phyl and asking her again and again, "You are happy there, aren't you, love? They are kind to you? You're not being overworked? You do get enough to eat?"

Mary thought of her pigeons, crossing the Channel by now, if they hadn't crossed yesterday. *I'll show her,* she thought; *I can bring in money, too.*

After dinner, Phyl and Mary went up to their room and talked. The strangeness wore off, and Phyl was her old self again. She told Mary all the little details about her life at Wendon that she wouldn't tell a grown-up: about the room she shared with Ethel and Annie, the gossip in the kitchen, the strange habits of the rich.

"But don't you hate it?" said Mary. "Being told what to do all the time?" Phyl had just related how Annie had been scolded for chatting to a delivery boy.

Phyl didn't mind, but Mary knew she would. She'd be in trouble all the time in a place like that.

She told Phyl about Arnold Revell and the bicycle.

"Arnold Revell!" Phyl pulled a face. "He's dopey."

"He's not," said Mary. "Well, he is at school, but he's clever outside. I like him, really—but don't tell any of your friends, will you? I don't want Olive and

Doris and them finding out and making fun of me."

On Sunday afternoon, after Phyl had gone, Mary went to the loft. She thought that if the pigeons had crossed the Channel there was a chance that one of them might get home tonight. She waited outside till dusk, but they didn't come. Tomorrow, then. Early, with any luck. If only she didn't have to go to school! The minute a pigeon landed it must be caught, basketed, and taken straight to the club to have its race ring taken off and put in the clock. But if Mary was at school, and Mum wasn't watching—well, it wouldn't be the first bird that had lost a race through not being caught quickly.

"Oh, stop worrying," said Mum. "Lennie's here. He'll watch. And Uncle Charley said he'd come over first thing."

Mary thought of Uncle Charley with his gray complexion and wheezy breath.

"But he can't run," she said. "He'll need to run, to get her to the club." She said "her," because she was sure that Speedwell would be the first bird home.

Mum laughed. "I'll run, if I have to. I'd run anywhere for a few bob."

And Mary had to be content with that. At least Mum was in a good mood. That was from having Phyl at home and being given her wages. But Mum was so changeable. The least thing might upset her, and then she'd be back to cursing "those damned pigeons."

Well, maybe Uncle Charley would keep her cheerful; she had a soft spot for him.

Mary was up and outside early on Monday morning. It was a fine day. The sky dazzled, making her squint with its bright emptiness.

"Come on, girl, get your breakfast," said Mum.

Hungry as she was, Mary went in unwillingly, ate while watching the window, and dashed out again.

She heard Uncle Charley making his slow way up the passage.

"Nothing yet," she said, as he came into the yard.

The sky was blank. Mary stared. Uncle Charley stared. Lennie stared and chattered and thought every passing sparrow was a pigeon.

"Now don't let Lennie jump up and down if she comes in," warned Uncle Charley. "Keep still. Don't scare her off."

They stared. The minutes passed. It was almost time for school. Mum, standing in the doorway, jigging Doreen on her hip, said, "A watched pot never boils."

"True enough," said Uncle Charley. He got out his pipe and stuffed tobacco into the bowl. Mary smelled the familiar pungent smell of the tobacco as he lit up and took a few puffs.

And then she was there! Speedwell—it had to be her! One moment the sky was empty, the next there was a whirring overhead and down came a pigeon, folding its wings to land neatly on the alighting board and step inside.

Mary ran to the loft.

"Careful, now, she'll be flighty," said Uncle Charley.

"I know," said Mary.

She caught the bird deftly and brought her out.

"It's her," she said. "It's Speedwell."

Uncle Charley had opened the small basket. Mary put the bird in.

"You're a darling," she told her, as she fastened the straps.

"Now run," said Uncle Charley. "Let's see you go, Mary."

Mary ran. Down the garden, through the echoing passageway, out along Lion Street. Everyone would know she'd gotten a pigeon back. She pelted down the High Street with her chest burning, past the post office, past Coleman's, past Greening's, past the sweet shop where Olive's face appeared at a first-floor window; down the bottom of the High Street she ran, and arrived, rosy and breathless, at the back door of the Rose and Crown.

Reg White, the club secretary, was there, as well as the other committee members. The clock was on the table, waiting. There was no other basket to be seen, no sign of another bird.

"Here's Speedwell," gasped Mary. She handed in the basket.

Reg smiled. "You're the first one in, young Mary," he said.

He took the race ring off Speedwell's leg and put it into the clock to record her time.

"She's probably won in Culverton, then, hasn't she?" Mary said. "What about the region?"

"Now, you know I can't tell yet. They all fly to different lofts, so we have to work out her actual speed in yards per minute. But she's made good time. Keep your fingers crossed, eh?"

Chapter Eight

Speedwell did win. She was first in Culverton and first in the region. It was Mary's moment of triumph, handing over her winnings to Mum, hearing Uncle Charley tell Mum how good she was with the birds, what a keen eye for form she had.

She took advantage of it soon enough.

"Those young birds," she said next Friday. "They need training. I could take them out tomorrow. Give them a toss."

Mum hesitated; Mary knew she was thinking of a list of chores. Then, "Take Lennie, will you?" she said. "He does get under my feet."

Mary packed some bread and jam and got Lennie washed and dressed and out of the house early on Saturday morning. She kept him out all day and brought him back, tired and contented and chattering about pigeons at supper time.

Mum was singing when they came in—a sure sign that she had had a good day. Doreen was upstairs, asleep.

"I could take him out again, next Saturday, if you want," Mary offered.

"All right," said Mum.

On Monday Arnold Revell passed Mary in the school corridor and muttered, "Done that bike."

This time none of Mary's friends heard him: she was grateful, then ashamed of herself. "I'll come tonight," she said.

The bicycle was unrecognizable as the rusty thing Mary had seen lying among the nettles. Arnold had straightened the wheels, fixed the chain and handlebars, given it a new saddle, and polished it all up.

"Can I really have it, for nothing?" asked Mary.

"Two pigeons," said Arnold.

Mary climbed awkwardly onto the bicycle. She couldn't ride it. She wobbled around the Revells' yard. Molly, Johnny, and several other small Revells stood watching.

On Tuesday, Mary went to Arnold's again. She told her mother she was going to Olive's. Mum didn't notice much. She was worried because Dad's money order, which should have come the day before, still hadn't arrived.

Arnold chased the younger Revells away and watched Mary as she rode around and around the yard until she could do it without falling off.

"Can I leave the bike here for now?" she asked. "Till I've told my mum about it?"

She wasn't sure how to tell her mother, so in the end she said nothing. The week was dominated by Mum's increasing anxiety about Dad. Every day, the mailman passed by the house without stopping.

"Something's happened," said Mum. "Oh, I wish he wasn't so far away!"

On Saturday Mary packed the sandwiches and the pigeons and set off again with Lennie, this time to the Revells'.

"I'll come out with you," said Arnold. "I've got a bike."

He sat Lennie on his crossbar, and Mary took the pigeons. They went down toward the river and then turned westward. Mary saw a signpost for Wendon and thought of Phyl. She cycled cautiously, a bit wobbly, careful of her pigeons. Arnold had to keep stopping to wait for her. When he came to the top of a hill, he sped away and went fast downward with Lennie squealing on the crossbar.

"Do it again," said Lennie when they came to the next hill.

So the journey was a succession of stops and starts, and they didn't get much of a chance to talk until they turned off the road onto some rough meadow land where Mary could release the pigeons.

"Where are we?" she asked. "Are we near Wendon? My sister works at the Hall."

"Wendon's over there," said Arnold, pointing to a smudge of trees in the distance. "See that bit of chimney sticking up behind the trees? That's Wendon Hall. This is Cheveley."

They trudged up the grassy slope, pulling their bicycles. Lennie ran ahead.

Arnold called sharply, "Lennie! Come here!"

Lennie stopped. Mary said, "What is it?"

"Quarry."

"Oh!" Mary grabbed Lennie's arm.

"It's all right," said Arnold. "Only the fence is a little broken."

They approached the edge. It fell away steeply, and the sagging fence had disappeared completely in one place.

"I've been down," said Arnold. "There's a little hollow space down the bottom; a cave, almost."

"Could we get down?"

Mary peered eagerly over the edge at the crumbling footholds. It was a long drop, and too steep for Lennie.

"I want to go down!" said Lennie.

"You can't. It's dangerous."

"Want to!" Lennie began to wail.

Mary thought quickly. "Let's have our sandwiches."

"Sandwiches," agreed Lennie. He forgot the quarry.

Arnold had brought an end of a loaf and some sausages; Mary's sandwiches were bread and jam. They sat down on the grass and shared it all.

The sun was hot. There were butterflies and bees among the flowers at the edge of the quarry. They could hear skylarks high up. The pigeons cooed gently in their basket.

Arnold picked a blade of grass, held it taut between his hands, and blew through it, making a loud harsh whistle. Lennie was impressed. He tried to do the same, dropped the blade of grass, blew a raspberry, and rolled around giggling. Arnold demonstrated again. Lennie rolled and giggled with delight.

Mary picked flowers. She found clover, buttercups, vetch, and trefoil, and ... "What's this?" she asked Arnold, interrupting a whistle. "Is it speedwell? It's growing everywhere around here."

Arnold stared at the nondescript little flower: mauve, pansy-shaped but tiny. "How should I know?"

"I thought you knew everything," said Mary.

"Not about flowers."

Mary looked at the flowers. They were something like the speedwell growing in her garden, but smaller, and not so blue.

"My best bird's called Speedwell," she explained.

"Daft," said Arnold. He was making a slingshot out of a plantain stalk.

"Daft!" echoed Lennie in delight. "Do it again!"

The pigeons were getting restless in their basket. Mary decided to let them go.

They flew better these days. They spent less time circling around, and gathered more quickly into a flock. Today they were heading east in no time at all.

"Let's race them back," said Mary.

She was joking. They had no chance of beating the pigeons. They dawdled on their way home, and arrived back in Culverton at supper time. Mary stopped to pick ragged robin and Queen Anne's lace in the hedgerows. Arnold showed Lennie rabbit holes and a fox's earth. They found a trap at the edge of a wood and Mary sprang it with a stick.

"It's cruel," she said.

"Girls!" scoffed Arnold.

When they reached Culverton, Mary took her bicycle back to Arnold's place and left it there. She found a furry jawbreaker in her pocket and gave it to Lennie.

"Don't tell Mum we went with Arnold," she said. "And don't tell her I have a bike."

Mum was in a more cheerful mood when they got back. She liked the flowers and put them in a jam jar on the windowsill. As she served supper, she said to Lennie, "Did you have a nice time? What did you do?"

Mary tensed.

Lennie said, "We went a long way. We found some squeaky grass."

He swallowed a few mouthfuls of soup, and continued, "Mary doesn't have a bike. We didn't go whee-ee-ee down the hills."

Mary felt hot. She began to talk rapidly about walking up Foss Bank carrying the pigeon basket. But she didn't have to worry; Mum was only half listening.

"I like going whee-ee-ee down the hills," said Lennie.

"Do you, dear?" Mum said. Her mind was on other things.

"I'll take him next Saturday, if you want," said Mary.

And she did. The next Saturday Mary and Lennie and Arnold went to Bugle Hill, and the one after that to Hazeley. And in all those weeks they heard nothing from Dad.

Most of the time Mum didn't say anything, but Mary noticed the change in her. She stopped singing. She grew thinner—the food was going to the children. The food changed, too. There was less meat, cheese, and bacon. Soon they were down to soup—thin, with cabbage in it—and potatoes and sago pudding to fill up on.

"I'll have to go to the Assistance," said Mum. "If he'd only write! Tell me what's going on."

Phyl's money, sent from Wendon at the end of the month, saved them from charity for a little longer. But it wasn't much; not enough to keep a family going. When it came, Mum went out and bought fish and chips—an extravagance, but heaven after the gray days of cabbage soup.

On the Tuesday after her trip to Hazeley, when another Monday had passed without the mailman calling, Mary went to see Mrs. Greening about a delivery job. She explained about the bicycle. "I'll be twelve on the twenty-eighth," she said. "I could start the next day. I could come when you want, because school vacation will have started by then."

"I don't know," said Mrs. Greening doubtfully, looking over her shoulder at her husband. "We've always had boys for deliveries. I was going to ask Bobby Lee."

"I'd be just as good," said Mary. "Better."

"I thought you were going to the fabric shop," said Mrs. Greening. "Like your sister."

"I don't have to do everything the same way as Phyl," said Mary. "Anyway, I know Doris Brown wants to do that, and she's twelve before me. I'd be good at the deliveries, honest. Better than Bobby Lee. And I could help in the shop, too—" she noticed what

74

Mr. Greening was doing at the back—"weighing sugar, and all that." Mr. Greening called out, "Give her a chance, Alice. At least she's eager."

"All right," said Mrs. Greening. She smiled at Mary. "Twenty-ninth of July, then. Three and six a week."

"Three shillings," said Mr. Greening.

Mrs. Greening looked at him sharply. "If the boys get three and six, so can Mary," she retorted.

Mary skipped home. Now she could safely tell her mother about the bicycle; Mum was sure to be pleased now.

But she was too late. As she came in, her mother, with a tight face, said, "I was chatting to Mrs. Mullen today. She was out on Saturday, visiting her sister, up Hazeley way . . ."

Mary felt herself blushing.

"You've been out with that Revell boy. Riding a bike. I can see it's true."

Mary began to explain, but her mother exploded. "Why didn't you tell me? Sneaking around like that behind my back. I felt such a fool, and Mrs. Mullen all surprise: 'Didn't you know, Mrs. Dyer?' I could have strangled her. It'll be all over Culverton by now. Why didn't you tell me?"

Mary's chin wobbled, and tears spilled over. It was a mixture of self-pity, disappointment at having her good news snatched away, and the realization that if "it was all over Culverton," people would be whispering behind her back at school tomorrow.

Her mother took the tears as a sign of repentance and softened a little. She began to nag instead of shout.

"It's the sneakiness I don't like, Mary. You can't be trusted."

"I can!" sniffed Mary.

"And I don't like that family, the Revells."

"Arnold's all right," said Mary. "Lennie likes him and—"

"That's another thing. Bribing Lennie not to say anything. How could you? Sneaking around behind my back ..."

"Arnold fixed that bike up great," said Mary.

"You can give it back. I'm not having you accept that—not from Sid Revell."

"It wasn't Sid. It was Arnold."

"Just the same."

"And I said I ought to pay for it." Mary explained about the pigeons. It was the wrong thing to say.

"Those pigeons!" her mother exclaimed. "They're the cause of all this trouble."

"It's not trouble," said Mary. "It's good. Mum, I've got a job. I've got a job for after school when I'm twelve. And I needed a bike for it and I've got one."

"What do you mean? I haven't spoken to Mrs. Coleman yet. And you don't need a bike."

"I'm not going to Coleman's. I'm going to Greening's. As a delivery girl. With my bike."

"A delivery girl? But we agreed—"

Mary lifted her chin. "No we didn't. Just because Auntie Elsie arranged for Phyl to go to Coleman's. No one asked me. Mrs. Greening wants me. Deliveries and weighing and helping at the back. Three and six a week."

That was Mary's trump card. The Colemans, who didn't need deliveries, would have paid only two shillings.

"Three and six," said Mum. There was reverence in her voice.

"Yes," said Mary.

Mum sighed. The steam had gone out of her. "I don't know what I'm going to do with you," she said. "You're—you're that different."

Different from Phyl, Mary knew she meant. Phyl wouldn't go around with unsuitable friends. Phyl wouldn't bribe her little brother with jawbreakers and tell lies to her mother.

"I'm sorry I didn't tell you about the bike," said Mary, looking at the floor. "I meant to. I kept putting it off."

"Well," said Mum. "We'll say no more about it. Three and six a week! Pity you can't earn it this week. I've only made a few bob from the mending; and it does tire my eyes in the evening. Once Doreen's weaned I can maybe leave her with Mrs. Lloyd and get a cleaning job, mornings, but right now ... You know, that money from your dad isn't going to come. It's three weeks now. He must have lost that job."

"Maybe it'll come tomorrow," said Mary.

But it didn't.

Chapter Nine

Mum went the next day to the Public Assistance Committee. Mary knew, as soon as she came in from school, where her mother had been. There was bacon frying in the pan, but her mother wasn't singing. She looked defeated. Her photograph—the one Mary loved—had been moved from its place on the mantelpiece to the kitchen table. Mum must have been looking at it. Mary picked it up.

"You can stuff that thing in the drawer," said her mother in a voice of suppressed anger.

"Why? I like it. You look lovely."

Her mother banged pots on the stove.

"It was all phoney, that. The hat belonged to my Auntie Ann. The parasol was one of the photographer's props. The trees weren't real."

"But you were real."

"I was then."

"You still are."

"But I'm not Adeline Hill, with her parasol and her dreams. I'm Lina Dyer, miner's wife, mother of six—two in the churchyard and three on Assistance. Three children at home and no money coming in except charity and the pittance I can earn. Oh, I shouldn't be talking like this to you! You're too young."

"Dad'll send something soon," said Mary.

"But where is he? Why doesn't he write?"

"Maybe he can't afford a stamp. If he's out of work again ..."

Her mother nodded. "That's it, I guess. Well, I've squeezed some money out of them at the Assistance, but it'll barely keep us alive. And whether it's worth the degradation ..."

Mary said, tentatively, "We're sending Speedwell to Bordeaux tonight, me and Uncle Charley."

"Pigeons!" Her mother's voice was bitter.

"They don't go hungry, do they? They're strutting around in that loft, all sleek and glossy, while we starve. Where does the money come from to feed them?"

"From Uncle Charley," said Mary. "But it doesn't cost much. And Speedwell—"

"I don't care about Speedwell," said Mum. "The best place for her is the pot."

Mary retreated. She put the photograph back on the

mantelpiece and crept upstairs. Speedwell could win, she knew; it wouldn't be much, but it could mean shepherd's pie for dinner one day next week instead of soup.

Later that day, when Mary came back from the railway station, her mother was more cheerful; she was nursing Doreen and telling Lennie a bedtime story.

Mary went upstairs. She found Bordeaux on the map and lay on her bed, gazing at it, imagining blue skies and the sudden uprush of thousands of birds. On Saturday they would be released. Le Mans had been over four hundred miles away. Bordeaux was over seven hundred. From there Speedwell would fly north, straight to Mont St. Michel. She'd hug the coast, then as far as Cap de la Hague. She wouldn't cross open water until she had to. But by Sunday night she should have reached Lyme Regis. Could she get back on Monday—maybe even late on Sunday? Could she set a record? "A record for Culverton Pigeon Club, maybe," Uncle Charley had said, smiling indulgently. But a nationwide record was Mary's dream.

By Saturday the money from the Public Assistance Committee was almost gone. "There were so many things we'd run out of over the weeks," Mum explained to Mary, as she served the baked potatoes and the soup with a few pieces of bacon in it. "Those people at the Assistance, they don't know what it's like." She put on a plummy voice: " 'Make sure the little ones have plenty of milk, Mrs. Dyer. And buy herrings; they're cheap and nutritious.' " Mary grinned. "What they don't realize is that before you're driven to crawling to them you've run out of bootblack, and string, and matches, and soap, and sugar, and lard ... oh, everything! There's nothing left for herrings."

"It'll be better next week," said Mary. "Now you've got those things."

"But they won't give me any more till Friday, and there's nothing in the pantry but jam and a crust of bread, and three and eightpence left in my purse."

"We could tell Auntie Elsie. She'd help," said Mary.

"No. I won't go running to her. We'll have to manage."

Uncle Charley came by first thing on Monday as Mary was leaving for school.

"Just to put your mind at rest," he told Mary. "Though you'll be home yourself before she is, I'm sure of that. They'll mostly come in tomorrow. Better, anyway, if they rest today. I think we'll have thunder before morning."

Mum agreed. "It's muggy. Thundery weather. So you've come to get under my feet, Uncle Charley?" Her voice was friendly. She liked having him around. And the mailman hadn't come yet, so she was still in a hopeful mood.

Mary spent the day thinking about pigeons. At ten-thirty, as the bell rang for the end of break and the children began lining up to go in, she was with Speedwell, resting on the south coast, gathering her strength for the long flight home.

"Go on!" Someone prodded Mary in the back. Miss Lidiard's class had been told to go in, and the three in front of Mary were going. She scuttled after them.

"Walk, don't run, Mary Dyer!" bawled bossy Miss Quimby.

I wish I could fly, thought Mary. *If I were a pigeon I'd fly over Miss Quimby and mess on her head*. The thought pleased her; she smiled.

"You can take that grin off your face, Mary Dyer," said Miss Lidiard as she came into the classroom. "You've done nothing but daydream all morning."

Mary glanced across at Arnold Revell, slouching in last from the yard as usual; she was beginning to know how he felt about school.

By the end of the day Mary was dreaming about food. She'd eaten her bread and dripping at lunchtime but it had seemed to go nowhere. *If Speedwell wins*, she thought, *we'll have meat tomorrow*. The thought sustained her as she ran home.

She met Uncle Charley coming out of the passage. He looked odd, she thought, ruffled. "Speedwell?" she gasped.

"No, love. Not yet. Mary"— he caught her arm as she turned into the passageway. "Mary, go easy on your mother. This is a hard time for her."

Mary looked at him, puzzled. "Aren't you staying? I thought you'd be watching with me."

"No." He coughed, leaning on the railings. "No. I'd better get home. Let you talk to your mother."

He shuffled off, and Mary turned into the passageway with a feeling of unease. Something was wrong; the conversation had felt strange.

A smell assailed her halfway down the passage: strong, rich, savory. Something she hadn't smelled for weeks and weeks. Meat. She ran indoors.

Meat! How had Mum managed to afford it? Mary stepped into the kitchen. Her stomach was begging for food. The whole kitchen was full of that glorious smell.

And then she saw her mother's face and understood. She felt cold. "Mum! Mum ... you didn't—"

Her mother turned away and brought a dish out of the oven. Meat. Brown, glistening, coated in dark gravy. Three mounded shapes. Unmistakeably pigeons.

The hunger drained from Mary. Fury took its place.

"My pigeons! You've cooked my pigeons!"

"Your father's pigeons," her mother corrected her. She was prepared, ready for battle. Mary, taken unawares, choked on her anger and couldn't speak.

"We've had pigeon before," said Mum calmly. "Your Dad doesn't give them an old age pension, does he, when they're past it? They go in the pot."

Mary found her voice. "But Dad chooses. Dad decides."

"And Dad's not here."

"But you don't know them! Which ones—which ones did you take? Did Uncle Charley choose them? Is he in on this?"

"No!" Her mother's voice was sharp. "Don't you blame Charley. He didn't know. Not till it was done."

Mary darted toward the door.

Her mother called out, defensive now, "Well, it won't be your best one, will it? That's in Bordeaux."

But Mary, running down the path, shouted, "She's not the only one. There's Ruby, and True Blue, and Bevin, and ... and the Gaffer."

The thought of the Gaffer with his neck wrung and gravy on him was worst of all. The Gaffer, who was so tame, who'd come to you as soon as you went into the loft.

She flung the door open, forgetting to be calm. Birds fluttered upward, startled; feathers floated down.

"Blériot ... Bevin ... Lavender ..." Mary's glance darted around.

A whir of wings, and the Gaffer landed on her

shoulder. Mary picked him up and began to cry. "I'd have killed her," she sobbed, "if it'd been you."

The Gaffer struggled. Mary let him go. She was calmer now. She looked over the birds, checking.

Ruby was gone. Beautiful Ruby, with her dark plumage and deep red eyes. Mum had snatched Ruby from her nest bowl and wrung her neck. Mary began to shake. The others were still there: Lenin, Trotsky, True Blue, Queenie ... Two of the young birds, hatched in March, were gone; two that didn't have names yet, that hadn't proved themselves—and never would now.

"If she'd asked," Mary sobbed, talking to the Gaffer, who sat watching from his perch with his head on one side. "If she'd asked, I'd have chosen her some." At that moment she believed this was true. "It wasn't for her to decide, coming in, grab, grab. I hate her!" She closed the loft and went indoors. She was still hungry, but the smell of the pigeons made her feel sick.

Her mother had served. There was a plate for her: potatoes, slices of pigeon. Slices of Ruby?

Mary gagged. "I can't eat that."

"You'll go hungry, then."

"You killed Ruby." Mary's voice rose. "Ruby!"

"I just took the nearest."

"You don't care, do you? Ruby had a squeaker, a baby. And you killed her."

"I have a baby, too. Your sister Doreen. Isn't she more important than a pigeon?" She turned to Lennie. "Eat your dinner, Lennie; don't cry. What does it matter, anyway? One pigeon or another? They're just birds."

Her logic infuriated Mary. "I hate you!" she shouted.

Her mother's face darkened. "Don't you dare say that!"

"You'd no right!" Mary went on. "No right to take them!"

Her mother turned on her. "I had every right, my girl! It's my job to feed this family; my job to find food. Lennie has the right to eat. And so do I, because if I starve, Doreen starves. If you don't want to eat, that's up to you. You can get out. Go up to your bed. Go on! Out! Upstairs!"

Mary fled. She ran upstairs into her room and slammed the door with a crash that shook the house. She sank to the floor behind it and sobbed noisily.

When her tears subsided she stayed sitting with her back against the door, hugging her anger. The smell of roast pigeon still hung in the air, tormenting her. Her stomach yearned for food; there was a pain in it. And there was pain in her chest caused by crying and anger.

I hate her, she thought. I'll leave home. I'll never speak to her again. But she didn't move. She hugged her knees against her chest and brooded as the sounds of dishwashing and voices came from below.

After a while she heard light footsteps on the stairs.
Lennie. He scrabbled at her door and pushed. Mary's
back resisted him. "Go away, Lennie," she said.

He didn't go. She could hear him breathing. He
always breathed noisily through his mouth.

"I want to come in," he said.

"No."

"It makes me cry when you cry."

Mary said cruelly, "But you ate them, didn't you?
You ate my pigeons."

There was a pause. Then, "They were nice," said
Lennie regretfully.

Mary heard her mother's step on the stairs and
stiffened. "Mary! Open that door!"

Mary unwillingly rose to her feet. She flung the door
open, confronting her mother with a rebellious stare.

Fear flickered across Lennie's face. Mary felt sorry
for him, but wouldn't soften because her mother was
there, still angry and unforgiving. She pushed past her
mother and ran downstairs.

"And where do you think you're going, madam?"

"Out!"

"Out where?"

"Anywhere!"

She went out, slamming the back door, and ran
down the path to the loft.

She took the Gaffer and put him in the little basket. She didn't know why she was taking him. It was not out of any great fear that her mother would kill him, but more of a feeling that she needed a pigeon with her, for comfort, and the Gaffer was the friendliest.

Her bicycle was kept in the shed now, where Dad's had been before he went away. She was hauling it out when her mother appeared in the doorway, her hands on her hips.

"When you come back in and apologize," she said, "I'll get you something to eat."

"I'm not hungry," Mary lied.

She wheeled the bicycle out of the back gate and noted with satisfaction that Mrs. Lloyd's net curtains were twitching.

"You won't get far," her mother said.

"I will!" retorted Mary. Ideas filled her head. Go to Stafford, find Dad. Live wild in the woods. Go to the seaside. Go and see Phyl, tell her everything. Yes. Phyl would see her side of it. She'd sort things out. Mary felt a rush of longing for Phyl.

She pushed the bicycle out and mounted it. Her mother still stood by the back door. Mary pushed down hard on the right-hand pedal and cycled away. She was still on Lion Street when hunger threatened to overwhelm her, but she couldn't bring herself to turn back.

Chapter Ten

She turned out of Lion Street toward the center of town. It had been a hot day, and the air was still heavy, but now she saw clouds darkening in the west and remembered Uncle Charley's warning about thunder. She should have taken a coat, she realized, as well as food. But she couldn't turn back now. Nothing would make her go back and apologize to her mother. She turned onto the road she had taken that first day out on the bicycle with Arnold and Lennie—the road that led to Wendon, and Phyl.

She cycled fast for the first few miles, breathing heavily, her anger giving her strength; but soon she began to flag. She stopped to pick half-ripe blackberries from a hedge and to snatch apples from an overhanging branch. Gradually she lost heart. It hadn't seemed far that day in June. But now, alone and hungry, with the temperature dropping and evening coming, she felt as if the road would go on forever.

There were few other people around. Occasionally she passed a countrywoman trudging along from one village to another. Twice a pony and trap came clattering up behind her; once a car went by a doctor, perhaps.

She knew she had to climb Foss Bank before she reached Cheveley. Every time she rounded a bend in the road she expected to see it ahead; the steep climb where they'd had to get off and push the bikes. But every turn of the road revealed another dull unfamiliar stretch, bordered by endless hedges, endless green verges full of flowers that didn't interest her now. Ahead, in the west, dark clouds were massing. There was an ominous yellow tinge to their undersides. It was going to rain soon—rain hard. She felt the expectant quiver of wind in the roadside grass.

The apples and blackberries hadn't filled her. She had to get food. And she was stuck here in the middle of nowhere. What could she do? Go home? Her pride wouldn't let her. Go to Olive's, or Uncle Charley's? No. They'd only tell her she must go and make peace with her mother.

Arnold's? She thought of the Revells' home: the dirty, casual kitchen where people wandered in and out and where there was always plenty of food: rabbit stew, big meat pies from the butcher's, hunks of bread. The Revells didn't waste money on shoes or shirts or soap, but they always had plenty to eat.

And they wouldn't ask questions. They wouldn't express shock or surprise or concern if she turned up there. Sid Revell wouldn't tell her mother where she was, or lecture her to apologize. She could go there, be fed and looked after, stay the night.

It was the thought of staying the night that checked her. She'd once glimpsed through an open doorway the room where Molly and the little ones slept. Mattresses on the floor, gray blankets, dust. And Molly, who always had lice, and probably fleas as well. She didn't care to sleep with Molly. Besides, her mother knew she was friendly with Arnold; she might come looking for her there and make a scene.

A drop of rain touched her face. Better go on, get to Wendon before it came down harder. She rounded the next bend, and there was Foss Bank. Wendon wasn't far now.

She climbed up the bank, freewheeled down the far side, passed the turning to Cheveley, and went on toward that area of trees where Arnold had pointed out to her the chimneys of Wendon Hall. The Hall lay in the shelter of the valley. For the first time Mary felt nervous at the thought of approaching the place. It was so huge, so totally removed from the world she knew. How would she ever find Phyl there?

Two immense black wrought-iron gates marked the entrance to a tree-lined drive. Mary didn't dare go in that way. She followed the wall around—miles, it seemed—until she came to a smaller, wooden gate. Tentatively she pushed it. It opened, and she found herself in a kitchen garden. A man in work clothes was hoeing between the rows of carrots and beets.

Mary's voice was small. "Please, I've come to find my sister. She's a maid here. Phyllis Dyer."

"You want the scullery door," the man said, pointing along a path. "Leave your bike. What's that you've got there—a pigeon?"

"Yes." Mary hesitated, her hand on the basket.

The man smiled. "He'll be safe here with me."

Mary propped the bicycle up against the wall and followed the path. She found the scullery door, but it was closed. The sound of loud voices, laughter, and a clatter of pans came from behind it. Mary hesitated. If she knocked, would they hear her?

Then the door was flung open, and a big red-faced girl bounced out, carrying a pail of vegetable peelings. She stared at Mary.

"I'm looking for my sister," said Mary. "Phyllis Dyer."

The girl put the pail down and stuck her head around the door. "Mrs. Coulter," she shouted, "there's a girl here asking for Phyllis."

Mrs. Coulter, in an expanse of white apron, her hair

93

in a formidable bun, appeared in the doorway and looked Mary over.

"I'm her sister," said Mary.

"I see."

Mrs. Coulter turned to the girl with the pail. "Get off with those scraps, Annie. Don't stand gaping."

Back inside, she called, "Phyllis! Your sister's here."

The next moment Phyl was on the doorstep. She looked tiny against the bulk of Mrs. Coulter, wrapped in an overlarge apron, her hands wet from washing dishes. After Mary's long journey and the strangeness of the great house, the sight of Phyl was so familiar and reassuring that she threw her arms around her and burst into tears.

Mrs. Coulter went back inside, leaving the sisters alone.

"Oh, Lord," said Phyl. She had turned pale. "What is it, Mary?"

The whole story came out: about the birds and Dad and the Assistance and Arnold and the bike and the fight with Mum.

"So I came to you," Mary finished. "I need you to help me."

"But—what can I do? Oh, Mary, I thought there'd been a death or something, not this. What can I do, Mary?"

And then Mary realized that Phyl couldn't do

anything. She had always thought of Phyl as the one to sort out problems, smooth things over, get her out of trouble. Phyl had been her big sister, confident and capable. But Phyl wasn't big here. She wasn't even a grown-up. She was just a little girl straight from school, a kitchen maid, the smallest and youngest of a houseful of servants. Phyl couldn't decide to put her up for the night or give her food—probably couldn't even give her any money.

"You'll have to go home," Phyl said.

"I can't! I want to find Dad."

"Don't be silly, Mary. You don't know where he is. You can't just run away. You must go home right now, before it rains and before it starts to get dark. What were you thinking of doing when it got dark?"

Mary realized that she hadn't thought at all. Phyl was right. She hadn't thought sensibly about anything.

"They'll have the police out looking for you if you don't get home," said Phyl.

Mary felt herself about to cry again. "Phyl," she said, "I'm so thirsty. And I've had nothing to eat."

Phyl looked at the half-open scullery door, bit her lip, and said, "You'll get me shot."

She went inside, and Mary heard her talking to Mrs. Coulter. A few minutes later she came out with a glass of water and a slice of meat pie on a plate. Mary drank the water almost in one gulp and gave the glass to her sister, who went back in to refill it. The pie was heaven. Mary was halfway through it when Mrs. Coulter came out.

"You finish that, and be off," she said firmly. "Go straight home. We can't take in waifs and strays."

Mary nodded, her mouth full of pie. "Thank you," she mumbled.

"How long did it take you to get here?" Phyl asked, after Mrs. Coulter had gone back inside. "It's almost sunset now. You must get back before dark."

"I'll be all right," said Mary. She had no idea how long it had taken her to get there, but she sensed that there was time enough to get back as long as she kept going. "I'd better go now."

"And you'll go straight home, right? None of this Stafford nonsense?"

Mary nodded, defeated.

The big girl, Annie, who had been loitering outside to hear what was going on, suddenly brought from her apron pocket something wrapped in a damask cloth.

"Here," she said. "There's three jam tarts in there. I stole them for me and the other two to eat in bed later, but you look like you need them more."

Mary took the bundle, hiding it under the cardigan.

"But the napkin?" she said.

"Oh, Phyllis can smuggle that back. You can give it to her next time she comes home." She gave a yelp of laughter at the sight of Phyl's frightened stare. "She doesn't know she's born, your sister. Me and Ethel are working on her."

The door opened and Mrs. Coulter snapped, "Annie! Inside, miss! There's work to do."

Mary sprang away, hiding her gift, and scuttled around the corner of the building. The last glimpse she had of Phyl was her sister's quick wave as she darted back inside.

The gardener was bending over his radishes. Mary slipped the damask-wrapped bundle into the front basket on her bicycle, wedging it next to the Gaffer's basket, and wheeled the bicycle briskly out of the garden and into the lane.

As she cycled up toward the main road, breathing heavily with the exertion, she felt the rain starting— not isolated drops now, but a steady patter. The air was colder, and all around was that weird yellowish light and the feeling of stillness before a storm.

Chapter Eleven

The storm broke as she was cycling back up the tree-lined hill toward Cheveley. The sky turned dark and unleashed lashing rain, forcing her to jump off her bicycle and run to the shelter of the trees. She stood there while rain blackened the road and beat on the leaves.

The trees gave shelter, but drops still penetrated. The Gaffer shifted in his basket, and next to him the cloth with the jam tarts in it was spotted with rain. Mary unwrapped it and ate the tarts while she waited.

When the downpour eased, she wheeled the bicycle out again and cycled up out of the valley and onto the main road.

It should have been lighter here, but the sky was so dark that it was almost as dark as the valley.

Mary cycled on, reaching the field path and stile

where she and Arnold had turned off that day to release the pigeons in the meadow. At that moment the sky was split by lightning, and seconds later she heard the thunder, a sharp crack overhead, followed by the hiss of rain.

Mary knew she had to get under cover fast. She saw rain falling in the distance over the hillside and sweeping toward her in sheets. There was another flash, followed almost at once by its thunder. The storm was overhead. She didn't dare go back to the valley; she knew better than to shelter under trees. But here, on the crest of the hill, she felt exposed to the lightning.

She looked around. Where could she hide? And then she remembered: that place in the meadow where a broken fence marked the drop into an abandoned quarry, and Arnold saying, "There's a little hollow space down at the bottom; a cave, almost."

A cave. That would be a safe place to shelter. She hauled the bicycle off the road and took the Gaffer's basket out. She left the bicycle propped against the hedge beside the stile. Once over the stile, she raced across the soaking meadow, feeling her shoes fill up with water. The rain beat on her head and shoulders. When she reached the quarry the sky was darker than ever and she could feel the electricity in the air.

The Gaffer's basket was going to make the descent difficult. Mary tucked her dress into her underpants, lowered herself over the edge, and began to climb down.

The rock was wet and slippery, the rain blinded her, and the basket bumped against her chest. She felt the sky flicker. Another crack of thunder resounded overhead. Mary groped for footholds and handholds. Slowly she made her way down; she was almost there. She shifted her grip on the basket, easing her cramped fingers. The Gaffer was a nuisance, but she couldn't have left him alone up there in the storm or let him loose in it. It was only then, as she thought of the Gaffer trying to fly home, that she remembered Speedwell.

Speedwell would be flying across southern England now, caught in this storm. There's going to be a smash, Mary thought. She pictured the pigeons, lost, disoriented, scattered by the weather. She'd lose Speedwell; they'd all lose their birds. The race would be a disaster. And as that thought came to her, the piece of rock she was holding on to came away in her hand.

Mary fell backward. She saw the ground only a few feet away and jumped down, landing off balance on the stony ground. Her right ankle twisted under her and she felt a sharp pain. She dropped the basket and rolled over, clutching her ankle.

She looked up. The quarry wall towered above her. It was difficult to imagine how she had gotten down, and impossible to imagine getting up again.

High above, the grass at the rim of the quarry glinted as the lightning flashed again, and when the thunder banged, it seemed to shatter the sky and release a torrent of rain.

Mary looked around for Arnold's cave. It was nearby—a hollow space under an overhang of rock. She picked up the basket, limped toward it, and crawled in.

The space was just big enough to sit in, and on another day Mary knew she would have enjoyed it: a secret place to sit and watch and think. But now she twisted about, trying to make her injured ankle comfortable. There was nothing to watch but the rain falling, nothing to think about but Speedwell battling home in the storm.

A summer storm. Unpredictable. Especially from France, nearly three days ago. That was always the risk with the long distance races. They'd have held the birds back, of course, kept them in the baskets, if a storm had been predicted in France on Saturday. But bad weather so near the end of the race ... She knew there would be people all over the country now, looking out at the storm, fearing a smash. There had been times when out of a thousand birds caught in a storm, only twenty-odd had come home.

Mary began to shiver. She crouched back into the hollow and sat with her arms crossed and shoulders hunched. The storm flickered overhead and the rain hissed down, steady, unrelenting. She saw that the sun had set; darkness was gathering in the circle of the quarry. Not just the yellow-purple storm darkness, but the true darkness of night. She was trapped here; she would have to stay all night.

Unless they came looking for her—the police, or whomever her mother might have told. But no one knew where she had gone. And besides, her mother might not have told anyone yet. She'd think Mary had gone to Olive's or Uncle Charley's or even to Arnold Revell's. There was no reason anyone should be worrying about her. Except Phyl, of course. But Phyl couldn't do anything. *I might never get home*, Mary thought. *I can't climb out. I've got no water and no food.* She wondered how long you could live without food. She remembered hearing that you could last a while—but not without water. She imagined the police searching for days, eventually finding her bicycle by the stile, climbing down to discover her corpse and bringing it home to her mother. She saw her mother weeping at the graveside, saying, "Poor Mary—if only I'd been kinder to her." The picture gave Mary a certain satisfaction. But it didn't warm her—she faced the prospect of a night alone in a quarry without a coat and with a sprained ankle.

Well, not quite alone. She took the Gaffer out of his basket and held him. She loved his sleek neck and his bright brown eyes and darting glance, his tameness. He pecked at a snagged end of wool on her cardigan and unraveled several stitches.

I could send you with a message, Mary thought. *Not now, but when the storm is over. You'd be home in no time.*

It was a shame to lose the vision of her mother weeping over her coffin, but all the same Mary felt cheered at the thought of rescue. Briefly, she even felt warmer. But it was quite dark now, and the storm was still rumbling. She'd have to wait till morning. She put the Gaffer back in his basket and leaned against the rock wall and tried to sleep.

The night seemed endless. She got cramped and woke up frequently to shift position. She was cold— miserably cold. Her ankle swelled. She kept feeling it in the darkness, comparing it with the other one. It throbbed with pain.

The lightning gradually ceased, the thunder rolled away, the rain lessened. But still Mary couldn't sleep well.

At last the sky grew lighter. She heard birds singing. The rain had stopped.

She stood up. The throbbing in her injured ankle was worse. She moved slowly, putting her weight on her good leg. Her mouth felt dry. She went out and wet her hands on the dewy grass and sucked them.

The sun rose above the lip of the quarry and shone

on the opposite wall. Mary picked up the Gaffer's basket and limped across to find a patch of gold.

The feel of the sunlight was like a shawl around her shoulders. The Gaffer was restless. Mary picked chickweed with dew on it for him to eat.

"You can fly home now," she said. "You can take a message for me."

And it was only then, as she said it, that she realized she had no pencil, no paper, nothing to write a message with.

Chapter Twelve

She could write on her handkerchief, she thought. But what with? She found a piece of chalky stone and wrote "Mary" on a rock; but the stone wouldn't write on cloth. There was nothing here that would do. She couldn't write, she decided; she'd have to send something—something that would tell whoever found it where she was. Something light and small. A plant? Suddenly she remembered finding the speedwell in the meadow at the top—a speedwell she'd told Arnold was different from the one in her garden. If she could send some speedwell, and if Mum or Lennie found it, and if they thought of asking Arnold what it might mean, Arnold might remember. There were so many ifs, but it seemed her only chance.

She had to search for a while before she found what she was looking for: a nondescript plant with tiny mauve flowers. She unraveled a little more of the wool that the Gaffer had pulled from her cardigan and broke it off. Then she took the Gaffer out of his basket and used it to tie a flowering stem of speedwell to his leg, tucking the end securely under his ring. She held him, reluctant now to let him go.

"You're the only company I've got," she said.

The Gaffer cooed. He darted his head forward and tweaked at her cardigan again.

Mary laughed. "You're making a hole. Silly old thing. I'll have to let you go. You'll fly fast, won't you? Bring me help soon?"

She put him down beside the basket and was almost relieved when he didn't fly off. Then she began to worry. The Gaffer was an old bird; usually he never did much more than circle the loft. Maybe he wouldn't go home.

But at last he took off. Mary squinted, watching him fly up into the brightness. For a moment he circled around, a dark shape in the saucer of light. Then he was away, over the lip of the quarry and out of sight. He'd be home in no time.

Now all she could do was wait. She limped around, drinking dew and finding a few clover flowers to munch. Her ankle felt big and painful. Soon she was forced to sit down. She chose a sun-warmed rock and felt the sunshine steaming the damp out of her clothes and separating and warming the strands of her hair.

But she was hungry. And lonely. She missed the Gaffer. She wished he were still there to talk to and hold.

Slowly the sun left her rock and moved to another. By the time it was overhead, filling all the quarry with its warmth, she knew it must be midday. Surely they'd found the Gaffer by now? But maybe not. If they were looking for her, they might not even think about the birds; they might not have been to the loft ...

No one came. The sun moved across the sky, toward the farther rim of the quarry. The place where she had sat in the morning lay in shadow. Mary was hungry. Her ankle hurt.

And no one came.

The shadows lengthened. In the place where she had sat in sunshine in the morning, the daisies were closing, revealing their pink undersides. Suddenly, in her panic, Mary decided that she must get out, on her own if she had to.

She returned to the cliff. She must reach the top before night came again. She tucked up her dress, braced herself for the pain, and began to climb, trying not to put weight on her bad leg.

She got a few yards up the steep rock wall and then stopped, gasping, unable to move. She needed to push up with her right leg, and couldn't. She tried to cross over and use the left, but it was no use; the rock was so steep, the footholds so precarious, she couldn't possibly do it with only one good leg.

And now she couldn't get down. To get down would mean jumping the last few yards—unbearable to think of—or risking a slithering fall. The pain in her swollen ankle stopped her from doing either. She leaned against the rock wall, tufts of grass clutched in her hands, all her weight on her left leg, too scared to go up or down.

"Mum!" she shouted, through choking tears. "Mum! I'm down here! Help me! Someone help me!"

No answer. The wind rustled in the grass on the edge. Far, far up, skylarks called.

Mary again thought of dying. Only this time it seemed real, and the satisfaction had gone out of it.

"Help!" she shouted. "Help! I can't get out!"

And then, an answer!

Voices, people coming. A man's voice shouting, "Mary? Is that you?"

And the next moment a figure appeared at the top of the quarry: Sid Revell. Glancing back over his shoulder he shouted, "It's all right, missis! She's down here. Stuck."

*   *   *

Mary sat in her father's chair by the kitchen fire. She was wearing a clean dress, her hair was combed smooth, and her right leg, propped up on a stool, had been expertly if too tightly bandaged by Auntie Elsie, working with angry hands.

Mary's mother's hands had been angry, too. On her cheek Mary still felt the slap her mother had given her as Sid Revell hoisted her out of the quarry and onto firm ground. And then, before the shock of the slap had died away, her mother had hugged her hard enough to crack her ribs.

Everyone had been angry with her: her mother, Olive's mother, Mrs. Lloyd next door, Uncle Charley, Auntie Elsie. Especially Auntie Elsie. Uncle Charley had seen the Gaffer come home and found the sprig of speedwell on his leg, but nobody had known what it meant. Mum had put off going to the Revells'. She had been to Elsie's, Charley's, Olive Jennings', even Doris Brown's. She'd had a feeling that Mary might be at Arnold's, and in the end she had confessed this suspicion to a surprised Mr. Jennings, who had gone to the allotment—"Poking around like he thought we'd murdered you," Arnold told Mary.

Arnold had gone back with Mr. Jennings to the Dyers', just as nosy Mrs. Mullen arrived to say that she had seen Mary yesterday afternoon cycling off in the direction of Wendon.

"Phyl!" Mum exclaimed. "I should have guessed."

Then Uncle Charley had shown Arnold the speedwell, and Arnold had said, "I think I know where she is."

"When we saw your bike by the stile I knew I was right," he told Mary proudly.

He wasn't angry, of course, and neither was his father. But all the other grown-ups felt it was their duty to lecture Mary on how thoughtless, wicked, and inconsiderate she had been. The house seemed to be full of them, scolding and nagging.

"And all you could say, instead of 'Sorry,' was 'Where's Speedwell? Has she come home?'" protested her mother when they had all gone away.

"Well, I wanted to know. And Auntie Elsie wouldn't let me go and look. She said I had to put my leg up. Mum, this bandage is too tight."

Her mother knelt to adjust it. She sighed. "Uncle Charley says not to give up. He says that only one came home so far out of the whole lot from Culverton. But they'll come back slowly, over the days and weeks, he says."

Mary knew that was partly true. Some would come home, but not all. In a storm like that, most of them would be lost, beaten down, driven into power cables, have their wings broken—or just fall, exhausted, to die.

She sniffed back tears.

"You really love them, don't you?" said her mother.

Mary nodded. "I want some of my own—when I'm grown up. I want my own loft."

"It's a man's hobby."

"I don't care."

"Things will get in the way," said her mother. "Marriage, babies ... Do you know, when I was young, I wanted to go on the stage, to be a singer. I was good, too. Always in the plays at school and chapel. I used to imagine my name up in lights in the West End: Miss Adeline Hill."

"Why didn't you do it? You can sing. You sing lovely."

"I didn't know how to go about it.

"Yes, I could have. But somehow ... well, the family wouldn't have approved—I knew that. And I went to work in the paper shop, and then I met your dad."

"You should have done it—gone on the stage."

"Then I might not have had you."

That was a strange thought: not being.

Her mother said, "I'm sorry I killed your pigeons, Mary. I should have asked."

"I'm sorry I ran away."

"Scared the life out of me, you did. What would I have done if we hadn't found you?" She smiled. "You drive me up the wall sometimes. But I reckon we'll rub along together a bit better now than we used to."

They heard footsteps in the passage. Mum pulled a face. "If that's Elsie again—" and then she stopped and listened. She darted to the door.

Mary, too, recognized the footsteps. She was struggling to her feet when the door opened and her father walked in.

Chapter Thirteen

"Don't ever marry a miner, Mary," her father said.

He was sitting in his usual chair, sipping tea, while Mary's mother sliced bread and fried an end of bacon.

"I won't," said Mary. "I might marry a poacher—they're never out of work."

Dad laughed, the laugh turning to a cough. He had lost weight, and his face was grayish.

"I'll send to Elsie for some of her cough mix," said Mum. "Mary, can you manage to go upstairs and get Doreen? I can hear her fussing."

Mary climbed awkwardly up the stairs, enjoying her injury in spite of its inconvenience. Doreen was red-faced and grizzly. Mary picked her up. At once she stopped crying. She put a pink fist to her mouth and made sucking noises.

Mary guessed her mother wanted to tell Dad about

the pigeons and how Mary had come by her sprained ankle; she took Doreen to the window and pointed out trees, birds, a cat balancing along the fence, diapers flapping on the clothesline. Doreen chuckled.

When Mary came back into the kitchen with Doreen in her arms, her father was talking about how he had fallen ill and lost his job. He'd found another job, struggled with it, still sick for a week, then collected his wages and headed home.

"I'd had about enough of being away," he said. "I met Bob Lloyd in town on the way back. He says they're taking on more men over at Staveley Pit. I'll try there."

"Not till you're well, you won't," said Mum.

"And what'll we live on, girl?"

"You've brought a week's wages, haven't you? And when that runs out"—she winked at Mary— "I'll sing in the streets. Put my Sunday hat down for pennies."

"Seriously, though," said Mary, "it's my birthday next Sunday, and I have a job starting the day after at Greening's."

"And Phyl's home that Sunday," said Mum. "She'll bring her wages."

"Everyone's safe home," said Dad.

"Everyone except Speedwell," said Mary.

Everywhere there was talk about pigeons lost in the storm: talk in the shops, in school, in the pigeon club. Birds came home in dribs and drabs, some so badly injured that they would never fly again, and others so exhausted that they died. But Speedwell didn't come home.

Every day Mary scanned the sky; every day her father let the birds out for exercise and looked, when they came in, for an extra bird. But Speedwell didn't come.

"We've lost her," he said. "Don't worry, Mary. It's not your fault. You've got to risk them to have a chance of winning."

But Mary was not comforted. She thought of Speedwell, beating across the Channel, every instinct driving her on, all her heart and spirit bent on surviving, on reaching her home, her loft, her mate. Mary couldn't bear to think that somewhere on that journey Speedwell had given up, fallen, or been driven down.

Arnold's pigeons didn't take her mind off it, but they gave her and Dad something else to do. Mary had told her father about Arnold's wanting a pair of birds. Dad went to the allotment with Mary and helped Arnold with ideas for building his own loft and promised him the pigeons when it was done. Arnold was soon happily at work.

"He's quick, that lad," Dad said. "Soon learn the tricks of the trade, he will."

"Miss Lidiard thinks he's stupid."

"There's different kinds of cleverness," said Dad.

Word soon got around at school that Mary was friendly with Arnold Revell. She became aware of whispers and glances.

On the Thursday before the end of term she was in the school yard, sucking a mint and gossiping with Olive, Edna, and Doris. Arnold passed by, heading for the boys' end of the yard. Mary made a decision.

"Arnold," she said.

He stopped, a bit reluctant, eyeing the other girls suspiciously.

"Dad's chosen you two young birds. They should be good ones, he says. One of Bevin and Ruby's, and one of Trotsky and Speedwell's."

Arnold smiled. "I've almost finished that loft. Want to see it?"

"Yes. I'll come on Saturday, okay? With Dad. We'll bring the birds."

Edna said loudly, "There's a stench around here. You coming, Doris? Olive?"

Doris screwed up her face. She went with Edna. Mary saw Olive hesitate, and stay.

"Want a sweet?" Olive asked Arnold, holding out her paper bag.

The young pigeons went to Arnold's, school ended, and still Speedwell hadn't come home.

Sunday the twenty-eighth was Mary's birthday. Phyl arrived midmorning, bringing a present: a silky hair ribbon and a brooch from Woolworth's in the shape of a bird.

"A pigeon!" exclaimed Mary.

"Well, I think it's meant to be a dove," said Phyl. "Best I could do."

"It's lovely," said Mary.

There was a red purse from Dad with a threepenny piece in it, and a cardigan from Mum; she had been secretly knitting it with wool unraveled from two old sweaters. Even Lennie gave her a bag of aniseed balls and stayed close to her until they were all shared out and sucked.

In the afternoon there was to be tea at Auntie Elsie's as usual, but today Auntie Elsie had said they would have "a bit of a do."

Everyone was excited. A "do" at Elsie's meant a can of salmon opened for the occasion, thin sandwiches, and little cakes, all laid out on the white embroidered tablecloth and the painted plates with birds. Later, there was to be a bottle of homemade wine for the grown-ups and fizzy lemonade for the young ones.

"I'll play the piano," Auntie Elsie said to Mum. "And you must sing, Lina. 'The Lark in the Clear Air.' I like that."

"And Uncle Charley wants 'Roses of Picardy,'" said Phyl.

" 'Plaisir d'Amour,' " said Dad.

"I'll be singing all night!" protested Mum, but a

flush of pleasure came to her face.

Mum and Phyl scurried upstairs to get ready: Mum in her cream blouse with the brooch of china roses that Uncle Arthur had made, Phyl in a new dress she had bought with her wages.

"And there's something for you, Mary," said Phyl, handing her sister a parcel.

Eagerly Mary untied the string. She shook out a dress: cotton, printed with roses, with a pink collar and a pink sash. It was faded and well worn, but Mary loved it.

"Annie sent it—the girl I work with. You'll have to gather it in with the sash." Phyl tossed the dress over Mary's head. "Lord, it is long!"

"But I want to wear it," insisted Mary. "Today."

"We can tack the hem up for now," said Mum. "I'll do it while you see to those pigeons."

Mary twirled in the dress. It was pretty. And she'd have to take it in, not let it out.

"Tell Annie, thanks," she said to Phyl.

Phyl was fixing a shiny comb in her bobbed hair.

"She's all right, that Annie," she said.

Mary put her old dress back on and went out with Dad to check the pigeons.

It was late afternoon, warm, with long shadows. The birds had had their exercise. They were all inside, and from the loft came a deep, soft cooing. Dad opened the door and went in. Mary, about to follow, heard a whirring of wings overhead.

She looked up.

A pigeon. Blue. A blue checker. It was . . . it had to
be . . . Speedwell folded her wings and dropped down
into the loft.

ANN TURNBULL set *Speedwell* in a fictional town based on Madeley, England, where she currently lives. She is the author of many novels for children, but says that this one was the most difficult to write because it was the first time she began with characters, not plot.